Enoch Edwin Byrum

The Great Physician and his power to Heal

Enoch Edwin Byrum

The Great Physician and his power to Heal

ISBN/EAN: 9783337042127

Printed in Europe, USA, Canada, Australia, Japan

Cover: Foto ©Andreas Hilbeck / pixelio.de

More available books at **www.hansebooks.com**

The
GREAT PHYSICIAN
and
HIS POWER TO HEAL.

By E. E. BYRUM,

Author of "Divine Healing of Soul and Body,"
"Secret of Salvation: How to Get It, and How to Keep It,"
"Boy's Companion," Etc.

MOUNDSVILLE, W. VA., U. S. A.
GOSPEL TRUMPET PUBLISHING COMPANY.
1899.

PREFACE.

THIS volume was written for the benefit of those who are seeking a knowledge of divine healing, and for the encouragement of such as desire to take the Lord as their physician.

The work is so arranged and classified as to present the subject briefly, and enable the reader at a glance to get an idea of the contents. As it is largely an arrangement of quotations of scriptures it will be observed there are many repetitions under the different classifications for the purpose of more clearly presenting the desired information.

The books entitled "Divine Healing of Soul and Body," and "The Secret of Salvation: How to Get It, and How to Keep It" will be helpful in a further investigation of the subject.

With a prayer for the blessings of the Lord upon the reader and an inspiration of faith and power with God for great victory, peace, and joy through our Lord Jesus Christ, I remain

Yours in Him,

E. E. Byrum.

Moundsville, W. Va., Nov. 6, 1899

CONTENTS.

The Great Physician.

A TIME OF HEALING PROPHESIED.

ENTURIES before the ushering in of the gospel dispensation, the prophet Isaiah, looking down through the annals of time, foresaw the breaking forth unto the world of a light such as had never before been known. And as with a prophetic eye he viewed the beauties and realized the blessings of such a time, he uttered these prophetic words: "Say to them that are of a fearful heart, Be strong, fear not: behold, your God will come with vengeance, even God with a recompense; he will come and save you. Then the eyes of the blind shall be opened, and the ears of the deaf shall be unstopped. Then shall the lame man leap as an hart, and the tongue of the dumb sing: for in the wilderness shall waters break out, and streams in the desert. . . . And an highway shall be there, and a way, and it shall be called The way of holiness; the unclean shall not pass over it; but it shall be for those: the wayfaring men, though fools, shall not err therein. . . . The redeemed shall walk there: and the ransomed of the Lord shall return, and come to Zion with songs and everlasting joy upon their heads: they shall obtain joy and gladness, and sorrow and sighing shall flee away."—Isa. 35:4-10.

As the prophet foresaw those things surely his heart was made to rejoice. No doubt he longed to see that day, when God would not only come and save his people, but when the eyes of the blind should be opened, and the deaf ears unstopped, and the lame made to leap, and the power of God manifested in such a wonderful way.

———————•———————

IECY OF CHRIST THE HEALER.

ISAIAH in his vision of the future not only saw that there was to be a time of healing, but it was made known to him how it was to be done, and by what means. He tells us of one who was to come, and says: "He is despised and rejected of men; a man of sorrows, and acquainted with grief: and we hid as it were our faces from him; he was despised, and we esteemed him not. Surely he hath borne our griefs, and carried our sorrows: yet we did esteem him stricken, smitten of God, and afflicted. But he was wounded for our transgressions, he was bruised for our iniquities: the chastisement of our peace was upon him; and with his stripes we are healed."—Isa. 53:3-5.

Here is a prophecy of the Christ of the Bible, of how he was to come and suffer for humanity.

HIS BIRTH.

"For unto us a child is born, unto as a son is given: and the government shall be upon his shoulder: and his name shall be called, Wonderful, Counselor, The Mighty God, The Everlasting Father, The Prince of Peace."—Isa. 9:6. We not only learn these words from the prophet long before the birth of our Savior, but we find that they were true. The angel told Joseph concerning Mary his wife, saying, "And she shall bring forth a son, and thou shalt call his name Jesus: for he shall save his people from their sins."—Matt. 1:21.

When this child was born his star was seen in the east. "And there were in the same country shepherds abiding in the field, keeping watch over their flock by night. And lo, the angel of the Lord came upon them, and the glory of the Lord shone round about them: and they were sore afraid. And the angel said unto them, Fear not; for, behold, I bring you tidings of great joy, which shall be to all people. For unto you is born this day in the city of David a Savior, which is Christ the Lord."—Luke 2:8-11.

FULFILLMENT OF THE PROPHECY.

IT is unnecessary here to tell the oft-told story of the early life of Christ; but we learn that just before he began his public ministry John the Baptist went forth preaching that the kingdom of heaven was at hand, warning all men to repent and believe on the Christ who was to come. Before Christ began his ministry he was led into the wilderness to be tempted of the devil, and there, after he had been fasting, and was weak, the devil came with great temptations, trying to lead him astray. But Jesus resisted him, and met him with the word of God, telling him what was written. But the devil also could quote scripture, until finally Jesus said unto him, "Get thee behind me, Satan: for it is written, Thou shalt worship the Lord thy God, and him only shalt thou serve." He gave him a strong rebuke by the word of God and gave him to understand that he would not yield to Satan's power and influence. This caused Satan to take his departure and flee from him.

Jesus then went about preaching the gospel and teaching in the synagogues of the Jews. "And he came to Nazareth, where he had been brought up: and, as his custom was, he went into the synagogue on the Sabbath day, and stood up for to read. And there was delivered unto him the book of the prophet Esaias. And when he had opened the book, he found the place where it was written, The Spirit of the Lord is upon me, because he hath anointed me to preach the gospel to the poor; he hath sent me to heal the broken-hearted, to preach deliverance to the captives, and recovering of sight to the blind, to set at liberty them that are bruised, to preach the acceptable year of the Lord. And he closed the book, and he gave it again to the minister, and sat down. And the eyes of all them that were in the synagogue were fastened on him. And he began to say unto them, This day is this scripture fulfilled in your ears."—Luke 4:16-21. "When the even was come, they brought unto him many that were possessed with devils: and he cast out the spirits with his word, and healed all that were sick: that it might be fulfilled which was spoken by Esaias the prophet, saying, Himself took our infirmities, and bare our sicknesses."—Matt. 8:16, 17.

Peter says, "Christ also suffered for us, leaving us an example, that ye should follow his steps: who did no sin, neither was guile found in his mouth: who, when he was reviled, reviled not again; when he suffered, he threatened not; but committed himself to him that judgeth righteously: who his own self bare our sins in his own body on the tree, that we, being dead to sins, should live unto righteousness: by whose stripes ye were healed."—1 Pet. 2:21-24.

JESUS HAD THE POWER OF HEALING

He not only had power to save people from their sins, but to heal them of their sicknesses, and remove their diseases, and loose them from the binding powers of Satan. Hear his own words, "All power is given unto me in heaven and in earth."—Matt. 28:18. Filled with compassion, he looked upon the multitudes and taught them the way of everlasting life, healed their sick, and cast devils out of many. He showed his great compassion to Mary Magdalene, to the woman by the well, and to the poor unfortunate ones wherever he found them, the same as to the rich man Zaccheus and others of high rank—he extended alike to all classes his love and tender compassion. Money could not purchase these blessings from him, neither fame nor flattery could lead him into an exalted position among the people, persecution and hatred could not turn him away from the poor; but he extended the privilege of salvation and healing unto all that would come to him in faith believing.

HE EXERCISED THE POWER OF HEALING.

"And Jesus went about all Galilee, teaching in their synagogues, and preaching the gospel of the kingdom, and healing all manner of sickness and all manner of disease among the people. And his fame went throughout all Syria: and they brought unto him all sick people that were taken with divers diseases and torments, and those which were possessed with devils, and those which were lunatic, and those that had the palsy; and he healed them. And there followed him great multitudes of people from Galilee, and from Decapolis, and from Jerusalem, and from Judea, and from beyond Jordan."—Matt. 4:23-25.

"When the even was come, they brought unto him many that were possessed with devils: and he cast out the spirits with his word, and healed all that were sick: that it might be fulfilled which was spoken by Esaias the prophet, saying, Himself took our infirmities, and bare our sicknesses."—Matt. 8:16, 17.

"Now when the sun was setting, all they that had any sick with divers diseases brought them unto him; and he laid his hands on every one of them, and healed them. And devils also came out of many, crying out, and saying, Thou art Christ the Son of God. And he rebuking them suffered them not to speak: for they knew that he was Christ."—Luke 4:40, 41.

HE TAUGHT AND PRACTICED HEALING.

WE find by reading an account of the life of Christ, from the time he began his ministry, that he taught and practiced healing. It was not only necessary for the people to come and be healed, but they must understand the conditions under which they could be healed—they must come in faith believing. He preached in the synagogues of the Jews and set forth the gospel of the kingdom, and went about healing all manner of sickness and all manner of disease among the people. His fame was spread abroad throughout the land, and many came to him in all faith and confidence that he would heal them. As some would get healed, this would inspire others, and they would come unto him full of faith, and go away rejoicing and giving him praise and glory. We can scarcely read of any place where he went preaching the gospel that he did not also heal the sick. In fact his work among the people verified his own words and the words of Isaiah the prophet, which state that the eyes of the blind should be opened at his coming and the gospel preached to the poor. Luke 4:18, 21; Isa. 35:5. Great multitudes of people followed him in the desert, in the mountains, by the seashore, and wherever he went. It was because of the great love he had for humanity.

One beautiful thought to us is, as we read how frequently after the power of God was manifested in the healing of the sick, and a great work was done through him, that he withdrew from the multitude and went alone to pray. Here, weary from excessive toil, he offered up prayer and praise and thanksgiving to the Father. Instead of remaining among the multitudes, where he might have received great honor and praise, he chose rather to be alone in communion with his heavenly Father, and there, in all humility and meekness, set us an example which should not be forgotten. He was not seeking fame—was not seeking honor of men—but sought only to glorify his Father in heaven.

HE GAVE THAT POWER TO THE TWELVE.

"AND Jesus, walking by the sea of Galilee, saw two brethren, Simon called Peter, and Andrew his brother, casting a net into the sea; for they were fishers. And he saith unto them, Follow me, and I will make you fishers of men. And they straighway left their nets, and followed him. And going on from thence, he saw other two brethren, James the son of Zebedee, and John his brother, in a ship with Zebedee their father, mending their nets; and he called them. And they immediately left the ship and their father, and followed him."—Matt. 4 :18-22.

It was not always among the highest rank of society that Jesus saw fit to make choice of those suitable for his work. As we meditate upon the word of God we see new beauties and the harmony of his work, and also how he fulfilled the word which says, "God hath chosen the foolish things of the world to confound the wise; and God hath chosen the weak things of the world to confound the things which are mighty; and base things of the world, and things which are despised, hath God

2

chosen, yea, and things which are not, to bring to nought things that are: that no flesh should glory in his presence. But of him are ye in Christ Jesus, who of God is made unto us wisdom, and righteousness, and sanctification, and redemption: that, according as it is written, He that glorieth, let him glory in the Lord."—1 Cor. 1:27-31.

These fishermen by the sea were not wealthy, were not educated men; therefore could not boast of their great possessions nor of their knowledge and intellectual ability; but they were men through whom the power of God could be manifested in a way that would be convincing to the people. They were not all fishermen; for "as Jesus passed forth from thence, he saw a man, named Matthew, sitting at the receipt of custom: and he saith unto him, Follow me. And he arose, and followed him."—Matt. 9:9.

"And when he had called unto him his twelve disciples, he gave them power against unclean spirits, to cast them out, and to heal all manner of sickness and all manner of disease. Now the names of the twelve apostles are these: The first, Simon, who is called Peter, and Andrew his brother; James the son of Zebedee, and John his brother; Philip, and Bartholomew; Thomas and Matthew the publican; James the son of Alpheus, and Lebbeus, whose surname was Thaddeus; Simon the Canaanite, and Judas Iscariot, who also betrayed him. These twelve Jesus sent forth, and commanded them, saying, Go not into the way of the Gentiles, and into any city of the Samaritans enter ye not: but go rather to the lost sheep of the house of Israel. And as ye go, preach, saying, The kingdom of heaven is at hand. Heal the sick, cleanse the lepers, raise the dead, cast out devils: freely ye have received, freely give."—Matt. 10:1-8.

THEY EXERCISED THAT POWER.

THE commission given the twelve disciples was one of power and authority. Before sending them forth he gave them power against unclean spirits, to cast them out, and to heal all manner of sickness and all manner of disease. He did not give them power to heal merely a few cases of fever, and certain kinds of sickness and disease, but all manner of sickness and all manner of disease. Their power was limited only by their faith in him. We read on one occasion where the disciples failed to cast out a deaf and dumb spirit, and they desired to know why it was that they could not cast him out. Jesus told them it was because of their unbelief. It was not because of a deficiency in the commission, or that they had exhausted the power which he had given them, but no doubt certain surrounding circumstances had hindered their faith insomuch that unbelief had crept in. Jesus told them that if the proper faith were exercised, nothing would be impossible unto them. Then he gave them some special instruction concerning the case in question, and said, "Howbeit this kind goeth not out but by prayer and fasting."—Matt. 17:21.

Before sending them forth Jesus gave them to understand that they must put their trust fully in him for all things, must look to him for the needed strength, for the words to speak when brought before governors and kings, for protection, as they went forth into the wicked world; and not only so, but he said, "Provide neither gold, nor silver, nor brass in your purses, nor scrip for your journey, neither two coats, neither shoes, nor yet staves."—Matt. 10:9, 10. Remember he said "nor yet staves"; that is, for the present they were not to take a staff, or walking stick. Mark tells us that he "ordained twelve, that they should be with him, and that he might send them forth to preach, and to have power to heal sicknesses, and to cast out devils."—Mark 3:14, 15.

What do we learn from this account of sending them forth in this way? Truly it is a lesson of faith and perfect confidence in him who sent them forth. He had promised to take care of them, and told them of the persecutions with which they would meet, and thus sent them forth in such a way that they could only trust in him for all things; and the fulfillment of his promises to them was convincing and strengthening to their faith. They went forth in this confidence and wrought mighty works.

But some time afterwards Jesus said to them,

"When I sent you without purse, and scrip, and shoes, lacked ye anything? And they said, Nothing. Then he said unto them, But now, he that hath a purse, let him take it, and likewise his scrip."—Luke 22:35, 36. They had fully trusted him thus far; now he could let them take their purses, their scrip, their staff, and whatever was needed for their journey, knowing that the Lord was fully able to help them in time of need. Thus they went forth, both before the death of Christ and after his crucifixion, with great boldness, power, and authority.

The healing of the lame man at the gate was one of the first healings after the day of Pentecost, and caused a great awakening among the people. "Now Peter and John went up together into the temple at the hour of prayer, being the ninth hour. And a certain man lame from his mother's womb was carried, whom they laid daily at the gate of the temple which is called Beautiful, to ask alms of them that entered into the temple; who, seeing Peter and John about to go into the temple, asked an alms. And Peter, fastening his eyes upon him with John, said, Look on us. And he gave heed unto them, expecting to receive something of them. Then Peter said, Silver and gold have I none; but such as I have give I thee: In the name of Jesus Christ of Nazareth rise up and walk. And he took him by the right hand, and lifted him up: and immediately his feet and ankle bones received strength. And he leaping up stood, and walked, and entered with them into the temple, walking, and leaping, and praising God. And all the people saw him walking and praising God: and they knew that it was he which sat for alms at the Beautiful gate of the temple: and they were filled with wonder and amazement at that which had happened unto him. And as the lame man which was healed held Peter and John, all the people ran together unto them in the porch that is called Solomon's, greatly wondering."—Acts 3:1-11.

This was followed by a very striking sermon delivered by Peter. The Jews became greatly enraged, and they laid hold upon Peter and John and cast them into prison until the next day, at which time they were brought before the rulers. Peter did not fail to testify clearly and positively as to what was done through the power of Jesus Christ. The lame man was there as a living witness.

"Now when they saw the boldness of Peter and John, and perceived that they were unlearned and ignorant men, they marveled; and they took knowledge of them, that they had been with Jesus. And beholding the man which was healed standing with them, they could say nothing against it."—Acts 4:13, 14. Thereupon the apostles were threatened and let go. They went to the company of saints and held a prayer-meeting, asking God to give them boldness to preach the gospel, that signs and wonders might be done in the name of Jesus. "And by the hands of the apostles were many signs and wonders wrought among the people (and they were all with one accord in Solomon's porch. And of the rest durst no man join himself to them: but the people magnified them. And believers were the more added to the Lord, multitudes both of men and women); insomuch that they brought forth the sick into the streets, and laid them on beds and couches, that at the least the shadow of Peter passing by might overshadow some of them. There came also a multitude out of the cities round about Jerusalem, bringing sick folks, and them which were vexed with unclean spirits; and they were healed every one."— Acts 5:12-16. "And they went forth, and preached everywhere, the Lord working with them, and confirming the word with signs following."—Mark 16:20.

HE GAVE THAT POWER TO THE SEVENTY.

"AFTER these things the Lord appointed other seventy also, and sent them two and two before his face into every city and place, whither he himself would come. Therefore said he unto them, The harvest truly is great, but the laborers are few: pray ye therefore the Lord of the harvest that he would send forth laborers into the harvest. Go your ways: behold, I send you forth as lambs among wolves. Carry neither purse, nor scrip, nor shoes: and salute no man by the way. And into whatsoever house ye enter, first say, Peace be to this house. And if the son of peace be

there, your peace shall rest upon it: if not, it shall
turn to you again. And in the same house remain,
eating and drinking such things as they give: for the
laborer is worthy of his hire. Go not from house to
house. And into whatsoever city ye enter, and they
receive you, eat such things as are set before you: and
heal the sick that are therein, and say unto them, The
kingdom of God is come nigh unto you.''—Luke 10:1-9.

In sending out these seventy we find he gave them a
commission like that of the twelve, sent them forth two
by two trusting the Lord for all things. And with
their instructions to preach the gospel they were also to
''heal the sick.'' And he further said unto them, ''He
that heareth you heareth me; and he that despiseth
you despiseth me; and he that despiseth me despiseth
him that sent me.''—Luke 10:16.

The Jews and people who so vehemently opposed the
work of the Lord, and looked down upon the apostle
and others whom Jesus sent forth, despising their presence and their work, little realized that they were
despising the Lord Jesus. So it is to-day. Many
people oppose the children of God as they go forth
fulfilling his will. Many people oppose the work of
God, and despise his people, not realizing that they are
thus despising Jesus; and when they turn away from
the truth preached by those whom he sends forth, they
turn away from the Lord himself.

THEY EXERCISED THAT POWER.

"AND the seventy returned again with joy, saying, Lord, even the devils are subject unto us through thy name. And he said unto them, I beheld Satan as lightning fall from heaven. Behold, I give unto you power to tread on serpents and scorpions, and over all the power of the enemy; and nothing shall by any means hurt you. Notwithstanding, in this rejoice not, that the spirits are subject unto you; but rather rejoice because your names are written in heaven."—Luke 10:17-20.

As the seventy went forth preaching the gospel under the commission received, they were almost astonished at the manifestation of the power of God through them; and when they returned with great rejoicing, telling the Lord how even the devils were subject unto them through his name, he assured them of the abundance of help they would have from him, and that they should have power "over all the power of the enemy." But that was not to be the cause of their rejoicing; they were to rejoice because their names were written in heaven. Their sins had been swept away, and they had been born of God by the Spirit, insomuch that their names were enrolled in the great class-book in heaven, which entitled them to the blessings of this life and the life to come, as they continued in his love.

HE GAVE THAT POWER TO STEPHEN, PAUL, AND OTHERS.

"AND the word of God increased; and the number of the disciples multiplied in Jerusalem greatly; and a great company of the priests were obedient to the faith. And Stephen, full of faith and power, did great wonders and miracles among the people. . . . And they were not able to resist the wisdom and the spirit by which he spake."—Acts 6:7, 8, 10.

"And there sat a certain man at Lystra, impotent in his feet, being a cripple from his mother's womb, who never had walked: the same heard Paul speak; who steadfastly beholding him, and perceiving that he had faith to be healed, said with a loud voice, Stand upright on thy feet. And he leaped and walked. And when the people saw what Paul had done, they lifted up their voices, saying in the speech of Lycaonia, The gods are come down to us in the likeness of men. And they called Barnabas, Jupiter; and Paul, Mercurius, because he was the chief speaker. Then the priest of Jupiter which was before the city, brought oxen and garlands unto the gates, and would have done sacrifice with the people. Which when the apostles, Barnabas and Paul, heard of, they rent their clothes, and ran in among the people, crying out, and saying, Sirs, why do ye these things? We also are men of like passions with you, and preach unto you that ye should turn from these vanities unto the living God, which made heaven, and earth, and the sea, and all things that are therein; who in times past suffered all nations to walk in their own ways. Nevertheless he left not himself without witness, in that he did good, and gave us rain from heaven, and fruitful seasons, filling our hearts with food and gladness. And with these sayings scarce restrained they the people, that they had not done sacrifice unto them."—Acts 14:8-18.

Paul was not one of the twelve, neither was he one of the seventy, but the Lord saw fit to send him forth; and he fulfilled the commission given, the same as did others whom the Lord chose for the ministry of his word. Before the conversion of Paul he was called Saul. At one time we find him a young man persecuting the church of God, consenting to the death of the saints. Jesus met him on the way and gave him to understand that in the course pursued he was persecuting the Lord. It was in fulfillment of the words of Jesus at another time wherein he said, "Inasmuch as ye have done it unto one of the least of these, my brethren, ye have done it unto me."

When this great persecutor of the church came to Jesus with a humble heart, repenting of his sins, he was forgiven, and was made a minister of the gospel of Jesus Christ, and went forth on his way glorifying the name of the Lord in word and deed. Now we find him at Lystra in company with Barnabas. A great miracle has been performed, like unto the fulfillment of the prophecy of Isaiah, wherein he says, "The lame man

shall leap as an hart.'' Through faith in Jesus Christ
the man was made perfectly whole, ''who never had
walked.'' The people were astonished. They consid-
ered that these brethren were gods, and were ready to
fall down and worship them. Paul gave them to
understand that he and Barnabas were not beings to
be worshiped, but said, ''We also are men of like passions with you.'' They were only men—were only
human beings, and not gods. He extolled the name
of Jesus Christ and urged them to put their trust in
the living God.

Again we find him among the Barbarians at Melita,
where a viper fastened on his hand; but his fervent
trust in the Lord enabled him to escape that injury, fulfilling the word spoken to the other apostles concerning
believers, wherein Jesus said, ''In my name shall they
cast out devils . . . they shall take up serpents; and
if they drink any deadly thing. it shall not hurt them;
they shall lay hands on the sick, and they shall recover.''—Mark 16:17, 18. Like the people of Lystra,
these Barbarians thought Paul to be a god. ''And it
came to pass, that the father of Publius lay sick of
a fever and of a bloody flux: to whom Paul entered in,
and prayed, and laid his hands on him, and healed
him. So when this was done, others also, which had
diseases in the island, came, and were healed.''—Acts
28:8, 9.

Paul also had the power to cast out evil spirits.
''And it came to pass, as we went to prayer, a certain

damsel possessed with a spirit of divination met us, which brought her masters much gain by soothsaying: The same followed Paul and us, and cried, saying, These men are th- servants of the most high God, which show unto us the way of salvation. And this did she many days. But Paul, being grieved, turned and said to the spirit, I command thee in the name of Jesus Christ to come out of her. And he came out the same hour."—Acts 16:16-18. "And God wrought special miracles by the hands of Paul; so that from his body were brought unto the sick handkerchiefs or aprons, and the diseases departed from them and the evil spirits went out of them."—Acts 19:11, 12.

While Paul was in Ephesus the people saw the manifestations of the power of God through him in the healing of the sick and the casting out of evil spirits, insomuch that some who were not children of God and were not commissioned to do those things, undertook to cast out devils in the name of the Lord Jesus. But they made a sad failure of it, as we learn by the following proceedings. "Then certain of the vagabond Jews, exorcists, took upon them to call over them which had evil spirits the name of the Lord Jesus, saying, We adjure you by Jesus whom Paul preacheth. And there were seven sons of one Sceva, a Jew, and chief of the priests, which did so. And the evil spirit answered and said, Jesus I know, and Paul I know; but who are ye? And the man in whom the evil spirit was leaped on them and overcame them, and prevailed

against them, so that they fled out of that house naked
and wounded.   And this was known to all the Jews
and Greeks also dwelling at Ephesus; and fear fell on
them all, and the name of the Lord Jesus was magnified.   And many that believed came, and confessed,
and showed their deeds.   Many of them also which
used curious arts brought their books together, and
burned them before all men: and they counted the
price of them, and found it fifty thousand pieces of
silver.   So mightily grew the word of God and prevailed."—Acts 19:13-20.

THAT POWER IS GIVEN TO SOME IN THE CHURCH.

"Now there are diversities of gifts, but the same
Spirit.   And there are differences of administrations,
but the same Lord.   And there are diversities of oper-
ations, but it is the same God which worketh all in all.
But the manifestation of the Spirit is given to every
man to profit withal.   For to one is given by the
Spirit the word of wisdom; to another the word of
knowledge by the same Spirit; to another faith by the
same Spirit; to another the gifts of healing by the
same Spirit; to another the working of miracles; to
another prophecy; to another discerning of spirits; to
another divers kinds of tongues; to another the interpretation of tongues: but all these worketh that one

and the selfsame Spirit, dividing to every man severally as he will. For as the body is one, and hath many members, and all the members of that one body, being many, are one body: so also is Christ. And God hath set some in the church, first apostles, secondarily prophets, thirdly teachers, after that miracles, then gifts of healings, helps, governments, diversities of tongues."—1 Cor. 12:4-12, 28.

THAT POWER IS GIVEN TO THE ELDERS.

"Is any sick among you? let him call for the elders of the church; and let them pray over him, anointing him with oil in the name of the Lord: and the prayer of faith shall save the sick, and the Lord shall raise him up; and if he have committed sins, they shall be forgiven him."—Jas. 5:14, 15.

When the Lord makes choice of any one for an elder in his church, he endues him with power from on high and commissions him with proper authority to fulfill his calling and office, in obedience to the word spoken by James, and also the admonition to the elders by Paul, when he said, "Take heed therefore unto yourselves, and to all the flock, over the which the Holy Ghost hath made you overseers, to feed the church of God, which he hath purchased with his own blood."—Acts 20:28. Whether or not an elder has the special gifts of healing, in order to fulfill his calling, he must at

least be so endued with power from above that he can
with unwavering confidence perform his duties among
the sick, as well as to care for the flock otherwise,
knowing that he is only an instrument in the hands of
the Lord, a servant of God upon which rests great responsibilities, whose works can be crowned with suc-
cess only in accordance with his perfect trust and confidence in the Lord.

THAT POWER IS GIVEN TO US IF WE BELIEVE.

WE now come to the word of the Lord and his
promises, which are brought down to us at the present
time if we are true believers. These promises are
given to believers, not doubters. The Lord has
never removed these pivileges from believers in his
church, and he never will do so. It is only as people
have departed from the faith once delivered to the
saints that they have been denied these blessings and
privileges.

In his last prayer to the Father, after praying for
the disciples who had been with him, Jesus prayed for
all who should believe on him through the word of the
apostles; and he says, "Neither pray I for these alone,
but for them also which shall believe on me through
their word; that they all may be one; as thou, Father,
art in me, and I in thee, that they also may be one in

us: that the world may believe that thou hast sent me. And the glory which thou gavest me I have given them; that they may be one, even as we are one."—Jno. 17:20-22. Truly we believe on Jesus Christ through the word of the apostles, as the gospel of the New Testament was written by them. Shortly after this prayer was offered, and just before his ascension, we hear him instructing his disciples: "Go ye into all the world, and preach the gospel to every creature. He that believeth and is baptized shall be saved; but he that believeth not shall be damned. And these signs shall follow them that believe: In my name shall they cast out devils; they shall speak with new tongues; they shall take up serpents; and if they drink any deadly thing, it shall not hurt them; they shall lay hands on the sick, and they shall recover."—Mark 16:15-18.

Notice here that he not only promises salvation to those who believe, but tells of the signs which shall follow them that believe; among the signs is, "They shall lay hands on the sick, and they shall recover." Again, Jesus said, "Verily, verily, I say unto you, He that believeth on me, the works that I do, shall he do also; and greater works than these shall he do; because I go unto my Father. And whatsoever ye shall ask in my name, that will I do, that the Father may be glorified in the Son. If ye shall ask anything in my name, I will do it."—Jno. 14:12-14.

Can we after reading all these scriptures say the day

of miracles is past, the day of healing is past? If so, we may as well say that the day of faith is past. But not so. The word of God is true. It is our privilege to be in the church of God, of which Jesus Christ is the head and builder, regardless of all creeds and elements of confusion. Then let us heed the words in Jude 3: "Beloved, when I gave all diligence to write unto you of the common salvation, it was needful for me to write unto you, and exhort you that ye should earnestly contend for the faith which was once delivered unto the saints."

FAITH WAS REQUIRED OF THOSE DESIRING HEALING.

"AND when Jesus departed thence, two blind men followed him, crying, and saying, Thou Son of David, have mercy on us. And when he was come into the house, the blind men came to him: and Jesus saith unto them, Believe ye that I am able to do this? They said unto him, Yea, Lord. Then touched he their eyes, saying, According to your faith be it unto you. And their eyes were opened; and Jesus straightly charged them, saying, See that no man know it. But they, when they were departed, spread abroad his fame in all that country."—Matt. 9:27-31.

"And a certain woman, which had an issue of blood twelve years, and had suffered many things of many physicians, and had spent all that she had, and was nothing bettered, but rather grew worse, when she heard of Jesus, came in the press behind, and touched his garment. For she said, If I may touch but his clothes, I shall be whole. And straightway the fountain of her blood was dried up; and she felt in her body that she was healed of that plague. And Jesus, immediately knowing in himself that virtue had gone out of him, turned him about in the press, and said, Who touched my clothes? And his disciples said unto him, Thou seest the multitude thronging thee, and sayest thou, Who touched me? And he looked round about to see her that had done this thing. But the woman fearing and trembling, knowing what was done in her, came and fell down before him, and told him all the truth. And he said unto her, Daughter, thy faith hath made thee whole; go in peace, and be whole of thy plague."—Mark 5:25-34.

To the ruler of the synagogue who came to Jesus for the healing of his daugther, when the report came that she was dead, and for him not to trouble the Master, Jesus said, "Be not afraid, only believe." He required the faith of the father to be firm and steadfast. When the man who was sick with the palsy was brought to Jesus by his friends, Jesus, "seeing their faith," forgave the man's sins and healed him. To those who have heard the word of God it is generally necessary that either the one who is sick, or one or more of his friends, have enough faith in God to call upon him for the healing, or to call upon the elders of the church or some children of God, to pray for him. It often happens that the one who is sick is unable to exercise any faith whatever, the friends have not the faith and power with God to pray for his healing, but can have enough confidence in God through his Word to fulfill the same by sending for the elders, or by having the children of God unite in prayer in behalf of the one who is sick.

SOME WERE HEALED THROUGH THE FAITH OF OTHERS.

"AND when Jesus was entered into Capernaum, there came unto him a centurion, beseeching him, and saying, Lord, my servant lieth at home sick of the palsy, grievously tormented. And Jesus saith unto him, I will come and heal him. The centurion answered and said, Lord, I am not worthy that thou shouldest come under my roof: but speak the word only, and my servant shall be healed. For I am a man under authority, having soldiers under me: and I say to this man, Go, and he goeth; and to another, Come, and he cometh; and to my servant, Do this, and he doeth it. When Jesus heard it, he marveled, and said to them that followed, Verily I say unto you, I have not found so great faith, no, not in Israel. And, I say unto you, That many shall come from the east and west, and shall sit down with Abraham, and Isaac, and Jacob, in the kingdom of heaven: but the children of the kingdom shall be cast out into outer darkness; there shall be weeping and gnashing of teeth. And Jesus said unto the centurion, Go thy way; and as thou hast believed, so be it done unto thee. And his servant was healed in the selfsame hour."—Matt. 8:5-13.

"So Jesus came again into Cana of Galilee, where he made the water wine. And there was a certain nobleman, whose son was sick at Capernaum. When he heard that Jesus was come out of Judea into Galilee, he went unto him, and besought him that he would come down, and heal his son: for he was at the point of death. Then said Jesus unto him, Except ye see signs and wonders, ye will not believe. The nobleman saith unto him, Sir, come down ere my child die. Jesus saith unto him, Go thy way; thy son liveth. And the man believed the word that Jesus had spoken unto him, and he went his way. And as he was now going down, his servants met him, and told him, saying, Thy son liveth. Then inquired he of them the hour when he began to amend. And they said unto him, Yesterday. at the seventh hour the fever left him. So the father knew that it was at the same hour in the which Jesus said unto him, Thy son liveth; and himself believed, and his whole house."—Jno. 4:46-53.

"And, behold, they brought to him a man sick with the palsy, lying on a bed: and Jesus seeing their faith said unto the sick of the palsy; Son, be of good cheer; thy sins be forgiven thee. And, behold, certain of the scribes said within themselves, This man blasphemeth. And Jesus knowing their thoughts said, Wherefore think ye evil in your hearts? For whether is easier, to say, Thy sins be forgiven thee; or to say, Arise, and walk? But that ye may know that the Son of man hath power on earth to forgive sins (then saith he to the sick of the palsy), Arise, take up thy bed, and go unto thine own house. And he arose, and departed to his own house. But when the multitudes saw it, they marveled, and glorified God, which had given such power unto men."—Matt. 9:2-8.

THOSE WHO PRAY MUST HAVE FAITH.

"AND all things, whatsoever ye shall ask in prayer, believing, ye shall receive."—Matt. 21:22. It is useless to pray unless we believe on the Lord Jesus Christ and his ability to answer; yea, we must believe more than this—we must believe that he hears us and does answer. "Therefore I say unto you, What things soever ye desire, when ye pray, believe that ye receive them, and ye shall have them."—Mark 11:24. "Without faith it is impossible to please him: for he that cometh to God must believe that he is, and that he is a rewarder of them that diligently seek him."—Heb. 11:6. "But let him ask in faith, nothing wavering.

For he that wavereth is like a wave of the sea driven with the wind and tossed. For let not that man think that he shall receive anything of the Lord."—Jas. 1:6, 7. The prayer must be one of faith, doubting nothing. "And the prayer of faith shall save the sick, and the Lord shall raise him up; and if he have committed sins, they shall be forgiven him."—Jas. 5:15.

THE DAY OF HEALING IS NOT PAST WITH BELIEVERS.

In the last commission that Jesus Christ gave to his apostles, when he told them to go forth into all the world and preach the gospel, he said, "He that believeth and is baptized shall be saved; but he that believeth not shall be damned. And these signs shall follow them that believe: In my name shall they cast out devils; they shall speak with new tongues; they shall take up serpents; and if they drink any deadly thing, it shall not hurt them; and they shall lay hands on the sick, and they shall recover."—Mark 16:16-18.

If the day of healing is past, then surely the day of salvation must also be past, as Jesus made mention of both at the same time. As long as there is any one on earth who will meet the conditions of true repentance, in accordance with the word of God, and put the same in practice in faith and confidence in God, just so long will the word of God be fulfilled in the salvation

of souls.   Likewise with healing.   Whenever people
meet the conditions of the word of God for the healing
of sickness and disease, with unwavering faith, God
will manifest his healing power; as we read in Heb.
13:8, "Jesus Christ the same yesterday, and to-day,
and forever."

ALL THINGS ARE POSSIBLE TO HIM THAT BELIEVETH.

"AND one of the multitude answered and said, Master, I have brought unto thee my son, which hath a
dumb spirit; and wheresoever he taketh him, he
teareth him; and he foameth, and gnasheth with his
teeth, and pineth away: and I spake to thy disciples
that they should cast him out; and they could not.
He answereth him, and saith, O faithless generation,
how long shall I be with you? how long shall I suffer
you? bring him unto me. And they brought him unto
him: and when he saw him, straightway the spirit tear
him; and he fell on the ground, and wallowed foaming.
And he asked his father, How long is it since this came
unto him? And he said, Of a child. And ofttimes it
hath cast him into the fire, and into the water to destroy
him: but if thou canst do anything, have compassion
on us, and help us. Jesus said unto him, If thou
canst believe, all things are possible to him that believeth. And straightway the father of the child cried

out, and said with tears, Lord, I believe; help thou mine unbelief. When Jesus saw that the people came running together, he rebuked the foul spirit, saying unto him, Thou dumb and deaf spirit, I charge thee, come out of him, and enter no more into him. And the spirit cried, and rent him sore, and came out of him: and he was as one dead; insomuch that many said, He is dead. But Jesus took him by the hand, and lifted him up; and he arose."—Mark 9:17-27.

Jesus did not tell the man who came to him that all things were possible to him if he doubted, nor to him that wavereth, but said, "If thou canst believe," all things are possible to him that "believeth." He left the bounds of faith unlimited. The man made a desperate effort to do away with his unbelief, asking God to help him, and with tears said, "Lord, I believe." His faith was honored accordingly, and his son was delivered.

WE MUST BELIEVE WHEN WE PRAY.

"THEREFORE I say unto you, What things soever ye desire, when ye pray, believe that ye receive them, and ye shall have them."—Mark 11:24. James says, "The effectual fervent prayer of a righteous man availeth much." Then he tells of a man who prayed for rain after a lapse of three and one-half years wherein it had not rained upon the earth. But when he went to pray he prayed with such confidence in God and such fervency that the prayer was answered. This man was Elijah. Even before he went to pray he believed that God would answer him. But he had good reasons to believe God, just as we have to-day, because the Lord had heard and answered him in times past.

It was only a short time before this prayer was offered when the priests of Baal had gathered together to offer sacrifices unto their god. There was an agreement between Elijah and the priests of Baal that they test their gods to see which were serving the true God, and the one which brought down fire to consume the sacrifice was to be the true God, the one whom they were to serve. Although there were four hundred fifty priests of Baal on the one side, and only Elijah on the other, it was such implicit confidence that Elijah had in the God of heaven that he suggested that they go ahead and offer their sacrifice first, which they did, calling upon Baal from morning until evening. But "Elijah mocked them, and said, Cry aloud: for he is a god; either he is talking, or he is pursuing, or he is in a journey, or peradventure he sleepeth, and must be awaked. And they cried aloud and cut themselves after their manner with knives and lancets, till the blood gushed out upon them."

But when it came time for the evening sacrifice, Elijah called the people together, repaired the altar of the Lord that was broken down, and placed the sacrifice upon the altar, and had them pour water upon it and fill the trenches round about; then he offered his prayer, and said, "Lord God of Abraham, Isaac, and of Israel, let it be known this day that thou art God in Israel, and that I am thy servant, and that I have done all these things at thy word. Hear me, O Lord, hear me, that this people may know that thou art the Lord God, and that thou hast turned their heart back again. Then the fire of the Lord fell, and consumed the burnt sacrifice, and the wood, and the stones, and the dust, and licked up the water that was in the trench. And when all the people saw it, they fell on their faces: and they said, The Lord, he is the God; the Lord, he is the God."

Do you suppose Elijah was afraid that the priests of Baal would be successful and he be defeated? Elijah had no fears whatever. With all calmness and assurance he awaited his time and went forth doubting nothing. We are serving the same God, the God of Abraham, Isaac, and Jacob, and we should go forth with the same confidence for whatever we stand in need of, knowing that he is able to do exceeding abundantly above all that we can ask or think, according to the power that worketh in us.

WE MUST HAVE CONFIDENCE IN HIM.

MANY people believe the Lord is able to do what he has promised, believe that he is willing to do it, but are unable to reach the point where they can believe that he does do it. Too often it is the case that people think it is for almost any one else but themselves. The enemy sometimes will make them believe that they are unworthy of the blessings of the Lord, or that their faith is too weak. Sometimes faith is looked upon as some great thing just beyond our grasp; but we must come to the Lord as a little child would to its parents, and remember what Jesus said—"Ask, and it shall be given you; seek, and ye shall find; knock, and it shall be opened unto you: for every one that asketh receiveth; and he that seeketh findeth; and to him that knocketh it shall be opened. Or what man is there of you, whom if his son ask bread, will he give him a stone? Or if he ask a fish, will he give him a serpent? If ye then, being evil, know how to give good gifts unto your children, how much more shall your Father which is in heaven give good things to them that ask him?"—Matt. 7:1-11.

Remember here that he is trying to show that we are to expect from him the very things for which we ask; and when we ask we must believe that he does hear, and when we believe that he hears us we must believe that he answers and that we do receive. "And this is the confidence that we have in him, that, if we ask anything according to his will he heareth us: and if we know that he hear us, whatsoever we ask, we know that we have the petitions that we desired of him."— 1 Jno. 5:14, 15.

HOW WE KNOW HE WILL ANSWER.

"BELOVED, if our heart condemn us not, then have we confidence toward God. And whatsoever we ask, we receive of him, because we keep his commandments, and do those things that are pleasing in his sight."— 1 Jno. 3:21, 22. "And if we know that he hear, whatsoever we ask, we know that we have the petitions that we desired of him."—1 Jno. 5:15.

In speaking to his disciples or to the people concerning faith, and receiving benefits from the Lord, Jesus always urged them to have an unwavering faith. The great promises given by him were if they would ask in faith believing—not doubting in their hearts. Or in other words, when they desired a thing they were to ask for it, expecting to get it. At one time he told them to "have faith in God." "For verily I say unto you, That whosoever shall say unto this mountain, Be thou removed, and be thou cast into the sea; and shall not doubt in his heart, but shall believe that those things which he saith shall come to pass, he shall have whatsoever he saith. Therefore I say unto you, What things soever ye desire, when ye pray, believe that ye receive them, and ye shall have them."—Mark 11:23, 24. "And all things, whatsoever ye shall ask in prayer believing, ye shall receive."—Matt. 21:22.

WHAT TO DO WHEN AFFLICTED.

"Is any among you afflicted? let him pray. Is any merry? let him sing psalms."—Jas. 5:13. The word "afflicted" means something more than sickness and disease. It includes sorrow and oppression on various lines. To the soul that is burdened with care and sorrow, to the broken-hearted who are weighed down with grief, to the weak who are oppressed, to those in ill health, who are suffering from the effects of the same with overtaxation of body and mind, to those who are buffeted about by the enemy, it is a relief to know that there is a place of refuge, a place where we can go and pour out our hearts and humble petitions to one who is always ready to lend a listening ear. We read the words of Jesus, where he says he was sent to preach the gospel to the poor, to heal the broken-hearted, to preach deliverance to the captives, and recovering of sight to the blind, to set at liberty them that are bruised. And again he says, "Come unto me all ye that labor and are heavy laden, and I will give you rest. Take my yoke upon you, and learn of me; for I am meek and lowly in heart: and ye shall find rest unto your souls. For my yoke is easy, and my burden is light."—Matt. 11:28-30.

Truly it is blessed to come to him who is abundantly able to deliver, and who will greet us with words of cheer, and direct us in the ways of his peace. For "there hath no temptation taken you but such as is common to man: but God is faithful, who will not suffer you to be tempted above that ye are able; but will with the temptation also make a way to escape, that ye may be able to bear it."—1 Cor. 10:13.

WHAT TO DO IN CASE OF SICKNESS.

WHEN Jesus was here upon earth the sick were brought to him, or they sent for him to come and heal them. At the present time those who are sick can not be brought to him in person, but we are taught in the word of God just how the sick can be brought to him. If able to exercise their faith, they can come to him in prayer in faith believing, and they will receive, in answer to their prayer, his healing touch; as we read in Jno. 15:7, "If ye abide in me, and my words abide in you, ye shall ask what ye will, and it shall be done unto you." But it sometimes happens that the one who is sick is unable to exercise the necessary faith. In such cases the Lord has provided in his Word and in his plan of salvation a means by which they can be healed. He tells us in Jas. 5:14, "Is any sick among you? let him call for the elders of the church; and let them pray over him, anointing him with oil, in the name of the Lord: and the prayer of faith shall save the sick, and the Lord shall raise him up; and if he have committed sins, they shall be forgiven him."—Jas. 5:14, 15.

Where there are no elders to be sent for, there is

another promise in Matt. 18:19, 20—"Again I say unto you, That if two of you shall agree on earth as touching anything that they shall ask, it shall be done for them of my Father which is in heaven. For where two or three are gathered together in my name, there am I in the midst of them."

It is not always that there are children of God present to unite their prayers in behalf of the sick. At such times a letter, telegram, or information may otherwise be sent to some who have faith in God. Many have been healed in this way. But even though a person is alone, he can, like Hezekiah of old, who was sick unto death, offer up an earnest prayer unto the Lord with tears; and it says, "Hezekiah wept sore." This earnest petition of faith and confidence in the Lord could not be turned away unnoticed; therefore the Lord sent a messenger to tell Hezekiah, saying, "I have heard thy prayer, I have seen thy tears; behold, I will heal thee." It is the earnest fervent prayer, the one that takes hold of the promises of God doubting nothing, that reaches the throne and brings an answer. It does not always require tears, but it does require that trust and belief that what God has said is true, and that what he has said concerning us is for us and our privilege to have. Prayers must be brought down to the present time. If we expect help from the Lord and find out our privileges, we must call upon him in faith, believing that he does hear us now. We must learn his will in the matter, and then believe for the fulfillment of it. The more active and definite our faith, the greater results, and the more speedy the fulfillment of his promise to us.

In looking to the Lord for healing in behalf of friends or ourselves, it is well to consider before the Lord our spiritual condition, and see that all is yielded fully to his will. It is sometimes the case that people are unwilling to die, and again some are too anxious to die, in order to be rid of the cares and responsibilities of life and depart to dwell with Jesus. Such things may be a hindrance to the healing. There are many things that may stand in the way of the healing power being bestowed upon the one who is sick. But where there is a perfect submission to the will of God in all things, and the Lord does not make plain that it is his will to take the sick one unto himself, it is our privilege to lay hold upon the promises of God for the healing and have the same manifested by his power. Above all things, when you are sick take it to the Lord in prayer. If you are a sinner, yield yourself to God as best you can; and if you are unable to know just how to yield yourself fully for the salvation of your soul, promise the Lord that you will do so as he makes clear unto you the way, and call upon him for the healing, and you can receive the healing touch, and he will give you light concerning the salvation of your soul; and as you obey him he will set you free both soul and body.

WHAT MUST THE ELDERS DO?

"Is any sick among you? let him call for the elders of the church." One who is not accustomed to trust-ing the Lord in time of sickness, who is not acquainted with the teachings of the word of God regarding the same, may wonder what are the duties of the elders when called. The word of God makes this very plain. It does not say that they are to bring their medicine-cases or give him a dose of medicine, powders, and pills, and such like; neither does it say for them to rub the sick with liniment, nor measure them, as the manner of some is, nor powwow over them, nor speak some mysterious words or go through some magical perform-ance, in order to charm away the disease and sickness. But let us read what the word of God says concerning the elders. "Let them pray over him, anointing him with oil in the name of the Lord: and the prayer of faith shall save the sick, and the Lord shall raise him up; and if he have committed sins, they shall be for-given him." You will notice the elder is to do his part in praying and anointing with oil, and the Lord is to do the remainder of the work, that is, to raise him up; in other words, to heal the sick.

There is another thing that the elders are not to do, and that is make charge for their services, as is the man-ner of the so-called Christian Scientists. When Jesus sent his disciples out and told them to preach the gospel and heal the sick, he said, "Freely ye have received; freely give"—as much as to say, You have had the gifts, power, and blessings of God bestowed upon you without money and without price, now use them likewise for the benefit of your fellow men. The elders especially should seek to increase in wisdom, knowledge, faith, and the gifts of the Spirit, according as the Lord may direct, in order to be useful and proficient in their calling, and "covet earnestly the best gifts."—1 Cor. 12:31.

THE PRAYER OF FAITH MUST BE OFFERED.

It was a prayer of faith that went up from the heart of the woman who touched the hem of his garment which brought the answer from the Lord, "Daughter, be of good comfort: thy faith hath made thee whole; go in peace."—Luke 8:48. It was the prayer of faith of the man who came to Jesus in behalf of his son who had a dumb spirit, when Jesus said, "If thou canst believe, all things are possible to him that believeth." The man cried out with tears, "Lord, I believe, help thou mine unbelief." It was a prayer of faith and repeated asking of the Syrophenician woman who came to Jesus in behalf of her daughter, insisting that he listen to her pleadings and grant deliverance unto her daughter. "Then Jesus answered and said unto her, O woman, great is thy faith: be it unto thee even as thou wilt. And her daughter was made whole from

that very hour."—Matt. 15:28. And we read in Jas.
5:15 concerning the elders, that "the prayer of faith
shall save the sick, and the Lord shall raise him up."
The Syriac Version of the New Testament reads as fol-
lows: "And the prayer of faith will heal him who is
sick, and the Lord will raise him up; and if sins have
been committed by him, they will be forgiven him."

WHAT IS SOMETIMES REQUIRED OF THE SICK.

"CONFESS your faults one to another, and pray one
for another, that ye may be healed. The effectual fervent prayer of a righteous man availeth much."—Jas.
5:16. If the one who is in need of healing is able to
exercise the faith, it is necessary for him to do so, like
the man that Paul perceived had faith to be healed.
"And there sat a certain man at Lystra, impotent in
his feet, being a cripple from his mother's womb, who
never had walked: the same heard Paul speak: who
steadfastly beholding him, and perceiving that he had
faith to be healed, said with a loud voice, Stand upright on thy feet. And he leaped and walked."—Acts
14:8-10.

The woman who touched the garment of the Lord
Jesus had the right use of her mind and was able to
exercise faith, and it was through her faith that she
was healed. "And a certain woman, which had an

issue of blood twelve years, and had suffered many things of many physicians, and had spent all that she had, and was nothing bettered, but rather grew worse, when she heard of Jesus, came in the press behind, and touched his garment. For she said, If I may touch but his clothes, I shall be whole. And straightway the fountain of her blood was dried up; and she felt in her body that she was healed of that plague. And Jesus, immediately knowing in himself that virtue had gone out of him, turned him about in the press, and said, Who touched my clothes? And his disciples said unto him, Thou seest the multitude thronging thee, and sayest thou, Who touched me? And he looked round about to see her that had done this thing. But the woman fearing and trembling, knowing what was done in her, came and fell down before him, and told him all the truth. And he said unto her, Daughter, thy faith hath made thee whole; go in peace, and be whole of thy plague."—Mark 5:25-34.

The two blind men who called upon Jesus had heard of his fame and were not afraid to believe on him for the healing of their eyes. "And when Jesus departed from thence, two blind men followed him, crying, and saying, Thou son of David, have mercy on us. And when he was come into the house, the blind men came to him: and Jesus saith unto them, Believe ye that I am able to do this? They said unto him, Yea, Lord. Then touched he their eyes, saying, According to your faith be it unto you. And their eyes were opened."—Matt. 9:27-30.

OTHERS MUST HAVE FAITH

WHEN the sick are unable to exercise faith because of not having the proper use of their mind, or from being weak or in great agony, then others must have faith for them, or aid them with their faith. We often read about those who came to Jesus, and he would sometimes tell them, "According to your faith so be it unto you," and where their faith was perfect and they came doubting nothing, declaring that they believed the work would be done, it was done. Again, there are cases like the blind man, who, not being so strong in faith, came to Jesus and received only a partial healing. This increased his faith insomuch that the next time he was prayed for he received a perfect healing.

A blind man once came to us for salvation and healing. His faith was very weak, and for a time he was unable to grasp the promises for either salvation or healing. After clearly pointing out the way of salvation, with the proper instruction, he was enabled to grasp the promise and receive the joy of pardon through the precious promises in the word of God. This gave him some confidence and faith, but yet he said he did not have faith enough for the healing of his eyes. We then told him that Jesus used to heal people according to their faith, and if he did not have faith for perfect healing we asked him if he would not make an effort to exercise what faith he had and be healed according to his faith, to which he consented. After united prayer had been offered for the Lord to heal him according to his faith, he was even surprised to know that the Lord had answered in such a manner as to do even more than he was expecting. Before the prayer he was in total darkness, not a ray of light could be seen, but after the prayer he opened his eyes and could name the objects we held before him, and even articles of clothing, and such like, on the wall at the other side of the room. While his sight was not immediately perfectly restored, yet he received such a miraculous work that he went forth along the street praising God for salvation and his great healing power.

In Mark 9:23, 24 we find one brought to Jesus for healing who was unable to exercise faith for himself, but Jesus required the father to exercise faith. However, he gave him encouragement by way of some precious promises.

In Jas. 5:15 we find the elders are to pray the prayer of faith. But even here some get the wrong idea; they suppose that the elders must do all the exercising of faith. While it is true that they must have faith and confidence in God, that they must be able to pray a prayer of faith, and in order for the healing to be done the prayer of faith must be offered, yet we can see even in the previous verse that the one who is sick, or his friends, must have faith. He must have enough faith in God and in his children to send for the elders, and must have such confidence likewise as did those who came to Jesus, to whom he said, "Believest thou that I am able to do this?" or, "As thou hast believed, so be it unto you."

In Matt. 9:2 is another striking incident of the faith of those who brought the sick to Jesus. In this case the man was paralyzed. He may have been so paralyzed as to have no ability to exercise faith, or may have been in a condition to join his faith with those who brought him; however, we read that as they brought him, Jesus, seeing "their faith," not only forgave the man his sins, but healed him, and bade him arise, take up his bed and walk.

WHAT MUST ACCOMPANY FAITH?

ALMOST invariably we hear the reply from those who have not learned to fully trust the Lord, saying, "Works! works!!—faith and works go together. Do all you can by way of medical aid and human assistance, and in case there is a failure, then put the case in the hands of the Lord." Or some say, "Render all the medical aid possible, and ask the blessings of the Lord upon the means used." But let us find what the word of God says about it. "What doth it profit, my brethren, though a man say he hath faith, and have not works? can faith save him? . . . Even so faith, if it hath not works, is dead, being alone. Yea, a man may say, Thou hast faith, and I have works: show me thy faith without thy works and I will show thee my faith by my works."—Jas. 2:14-18.

By this we see the word of God requires works to accompany faith. The next question would be, What are the works? We can not find one place in the New Testament where it says medicines and medical aid are the works required. Wherein instructions are given concerning sending for elders, we learn that they are to anoint with oil. This is not from a medical standpoint —not for the healing properties in the oil—but it is in fulfillment of the word of God; the same as it was with Naaman the leper, who was instructed to go and dip himself seven times in the river Jordan. There was no virtue of healing in the waters of Jordan, there was no magic in the number of times to be dipped, to charm away the disease, but he was healed because he obeyed the word of the Lord. The blind man who had clay and spittle put upon his eyes, and was commanded to go and wash, was not healed because of the clay and spittle nor of the washing, but it was because of his obedience.

Was not Abraham our father justified by works, when he had offered Isaac his son upon the altar? Seest thou how faith wrought with his works; and by faith was works made perfect? And the scripture was fulfilled which saith, Abraham believed God, and it was imputed unto him for righteousness: and he was called the friend of God. Ye see then how that by works a man is justified, and not by faith only."—Jas.

2:21-24. Here we find Abraham was blessed in his deed because of his unwavering faith in God. The Word says, "Abraham believed God." "He staggered not at the promise of God through unbelief; but was strong in faith, giving glory to God; and being fully persuaded, that what he had promised, he was able also to perform."—Rom. 4:20, 21.

Oh, could we at all times and in all things only believe God as Abraham believed him, and stagger not at his promises, how many more blessings we would enjoy and how we would see the fulfillment of his promises as our privileges in Christ Jesus! In fact, faith in God is only believing him—believing his Word. An active faith is putting into action or practice the things which we believe concerning his promises.

WHAT ARE THE WORKS?

Where there are faults, confess them. "Is any among you afflicted? let him pray. Is any merry? let him sing psalms. Is any sick among you? let him call for the elders of the church; and let them pray over him, anointing him with oil in the name of the Lord: and the prayer of faith shall save the sick, and the Lord shall raise him up; and if he have committed sins, they shall be forgiven him. Confess your faults one to another, and pray one for another, that ye may be healed. The effectual fervent prayer of a righteous man availeth much."—Jas. 5:13-16.

Works of the centurion—came to Jesus. "And when Jesus was entered into Capernaum, there came unto him a centurion, beseeching him, and saying, Lord, my servant lieth at home sick of the palsy, grievously tormented. And Jesus saith unto him, I will come and heal him. The centurion answered and said, Lord, I am not worthy that thou shouldest come under my roof: but speak the word only, and my servant shall be healed. For I am a man under authority, having soldiers under me: and I say to this man, Go, and he goeth; and to another, Come, and he cometh; and to my servant, Do this, and he doeth it. When Jesus heard it he marveled, and said to them that followed, Verily I say unto you, I have not found so great faith, no, not in Israel. . . . And Jesus said unto the centurion, Go thy way; and as thou hast believed, so be it done unto thee. And his servant was healed in the selfsame hour."—Matt. 8:5-13.

Works of the man with the withered hand—he stretched it forth. "And behold, there was a man which had his hand withered. And they asked him, saying, Is it lawful to heal on the Sabbath days? that they might accuse him. And he said unto them, What man shall there be among you, that shall have one sheep, and if it fall into a pit on the Sabbath day, will he not lay hold on it, and lift it out? How much then is a man better than a sheep? Wherefore it is lawful to do well on the Sabbath days. Then saith he to the man, Stretch forth thine hand. And he stretched it forth;

and it was restored whole, like as the other.''—Matt.
12:10-13.

Works of the lame man—looked and arose. "Now
when Peter and John went up together into the temple
at the hour of prayer, being the ninth hour. And a
certain man lame from his mother's womb was carried, whom they laid daily at the gate of the temple
which is called Beautiful, to ask alms of them that
went into the temple; who, seeing Peter and John
about to go into the temple, asked an alms. And
Peter, fastening his eyes upon him with John, said,
Look on us. And he gave heed unto them, expecting
to receive something of them. Then Peter said, Silver
and gold have I none; but such as I have give I thee:
In the name of Jesus Christ of Nazareth rise up and
walk. And he took him by the right hand, and lifted
him up: and immediately his feet and ankle bones received strength. And he leaping up stood, and walked,
and entered with them into the temple, walking, and
leaping, and praising God.''—Acts 3:1-8.

*Works of the woman with an issue of blood—touched
his garment.* "And a certain woman, which had an
issue of blood, twelve years, and had suffered many
things of many physicians, and had spent all that she
had, and was nothing bettered, but rather grew worse,
when she had heard of Jesus, came in the press behind,
and touched his garment. For she said, If I may
touch but his clothes, I shall be whole. And straightway the fountain of her blood was dried up; and she

felt in her body that she was healed of that plague. And Jesus, immediately knowing in himself that virtue had gone out of him, turned about in the press, and said, Who touched me? And his disciples said unto him, Thou seest the multitude thronging thee, and sayest thou, Who touched me? And he looked round about to see her that had done this thing. But the woman fearing and trembling, knowing what was done in her, came and fell down before him, and told him all the truth. And he said unto her, Daughter, thy faith hath made thee whole; go in peace, and be whole of thy plague."—Mark 5:25-34.

Works of the ten lepers—showed themselves to the priests. "And as he entered into a certain village, there met him ten men that were lepers, which stood afar off: and they lifted up their voices and said, Jesus, Master, have mercy on us. And when he saw them, he said unto them, Go show yourselves unto the priests. And it came to pass, that as they went, they were cleansed."—Luke 17:12-14.

Works of the blind man—washed in the pool of Siloam. "And as Jesus passed by, he saw a man which was blind from his birth. And his disciples asked him, saying, Master, who did sin, this man or his parents, that he was born blind? Jesus answered, Neither hath this man sinned, nor his parents: but that the works of God should be made manifest in him. I must work the works of him that sent me, while it is day: the night cometh when no man can

work. As long as I am in the world, I am the light
of the world. When he had thus spoken, he spat on
the ground, and made clay of the spittle, and he
anointed the eyes of the blind man with the clay, and
said unto him, Go, wash in the pool of Siloam (which
is by interpretation, Sent). He went his way, therefore,
and washed, and came seeing. The neighbors, therefore, and they which before had seen him that he was
blind, said, Is not this he that sat and begged?''—
Jno. 9:1-7.

*Works of Naaman the leper—washed in the river
Jordan.* "So Naaman came with his horses and with
his chariot, and stood at the door of the house of
Elisha.   And Elisha sent a messenger unto him, saying, Go and wash in Jordan seven times, and thy flesh
shall come again unto thee, and thou shalt be clean.
But Naaman was wroth, and went away, and said,
Behold, I thought, He will surely come out to me,
and stand, and call on the name of the Lord his God,
and strike his hand over the place, and recover the
leper.   Are not Abana and Pharpar, rivers of Damas-
cus, better than all the waters of Israel? may I not
wash in them, and be clean?   So he turned and went
away in a rage.   And his servants came near, and
spake unto him, and said, My father, if the prophet
had bid thee do some great thing, wouldst thou not
have done it? how much rather then, when he saith
unto thee, Wash, and be clean?   Then went he down
and dipped himself seven times in Jordan, according

to the saying of the man of God: and his flesh came again like unto the flesh of a little child, and he was clean."—2 Kings 5:10-14.

----—•--——

THE LAYING ON OF HANDS.

Jesus laid hands on the sick. "Now when the sun was setting, all they that had any sick with divers diseases brought them unto him; and he laid his hands on every one of them, and healed them. And devils also came out of many, crying out, and saying, Thou art Christ the Son of God. And he rebuking them suffered them not to speak: for they knew that he was Christ."—Luke 4:40, 41. "But Jesus said unto them, A prophet is not without honor, but in his own country, and among his own kin, and in his own house. and he could there do no mighty work, save that he laid his hands upon a few sick folk, and healed them. And he marveled because of their unbelief."—Mark 6:4-6.

He took Jairus' daughter by the hand. "While he yet spake, there came from the ruler of the synagogue's house certain which said, Thy daughter is dead; why troublest thou the Master any further? As soon as Jesus heard the word that was spoken, he said unto the ruler of the synagogue, Be not afraid, only believe. And he suffered no man to follow him save Peter, and James, and John the brother of James. And he cometh to the house of the ruler of the synagogue, and seeth the tumult, and them that wept and wailed greatly. And when he was come in, he saith unto them, Why make ye this ado, and weep? the damsel is not dead, but sleepeth. And they laughed him to scorn. But when he had put them all out, he taketh the father and the mother of the damsel, and them that were with him, and entereth in where the damsel was lying. And he took the damsel by the hand, and said unto her, Talitha cumi; which is, being interpreted, Damsel, I say unto thee, arise. And straightway the damsel arose, and walked."—Mark 5:35-42.

He put his hands twice on the eyes of the blind man. "And he cometh to Bethsaida; and they bring a blind man unto him, and besought him to touch him. And he took the blind man by the hand, and led him out of the town; and when he had spit on his eyes, and put his hands upon him, he asked him if he saw aught. And he looked up, and said, I see men as trees, walking. After that he put his hands again upon his eyes, and made him look up; and he was restored, and saw every man clearly."—Mark 8:22-25.

He laid hands on the crooked woman. "And, behold, there was a woman which had a spirit of infirmity eighteen years, and was bowed together, and could in no wise lift up herself. And when Jesus saw her, he called her to him, and said unto her, Woman, thou art loosed from thine infirmity. And he laid his hands on her: and immediately she was made straight, and glorified God."—Luke 13:11-13.

He touched the ear of the servant of the high priest.
"And one of them smote the servant of the high priest
and cut off his right ear. And Jesus answered and
said, Suffer ye thus far. And he touched his ear, and
healed him."—Luke 22:50, 51.

He touched the deaf man. "And they bring unto
him one that was deaf, and had an impediment in his
speech; and they beseech him to put his hand upon
him. And he took him aside from the multitude,
and put his fingers into his ears, and he spit and
touched his tongue; and looking up to heaven, he
sighed, and saith unto him, Ephphatha, that is, Be
opened. And straightway his ears were opened, and
the string of his tongue was loosed, and he spake
plain."—Mark 7:32-35.

Ananias laid hands on Saul. "And Ananias went
his way, and entered into the house; and putting his
hands on him said, Brother Saul, the Lord, even
Jesus, that appeared unto thee in the way as thou
camest, hath sent me, that thou mightest receive thy
sight, and be filled with the Holy Ghost. And immediately there fell from his eyes as it had been scales:
and he received sight forthwith, and arose, and was
baptized."—Acts 9:17, 18.

Paul laid hands on the father of Publius. "And it
came to pass, that the father of Publius lay sick of a
fever and of a bloody flux: to whom Paul entered in,
and prayed, and laid his hands on him, and healed
him. So when this was done, others also, which had

diseases in the island, came, and were healed.''—Acts 28:8, 9.

Peter raised Dorcas. "Now there was at Joppa a certain disciple named Tabitha, which by interpretation is called Dorcas: this woman was full of good works and almsdeeds which she did. And it came to pass in those days, that she was sick, and died: whom when they had washed, they laid her in an upper chamber. And forasmuch as Lydda was nigh to Joppa, and the disciples had heard that Peter was there, they sent unto him two men, desiring him that he would not delay to come to them. Then Peter arose and went with them. When he was come, they brought him into the upper chamber: and all the widows stood by him weeping, and showing the coats and garments which Dorcas made, while she was with them. But Peter put them all forth, and kneeled down, and prayed; and turning him to the body said, Tabitha, arise. And she opened her eyes: and when she saw Peter, she sat up. And he gave her his hand, and lifted her up; and when he had called the saints and widows, he presented her alive. And it was known throughout all Joppa; and many believed in the Lord.''—Acts 9:36-42.

The apostles laid on hands. "And he said unto them, Go ye into all the world, and preach the gospel to every creature. . . . And they went forth, and preached everywhere, the Lord working with them, and confirming the Word with signs following.''—Mark 16:15-20.

Them that believe shall lay on hands. "And these signs shall follow them that believe: In my name shall they cast out devils; they shall speak with new tongues; they shall take up serpents; and if they drink any deadly thing, it shall not hurt them; they shall lay hands on the sick, and they shall recover."—Mark 16:17, 18.

ANOINTING WITH OIL.

The apostles anointed with oil. "And he called unto him the twelve, and began to send them forth by two and two; and gave them power over unclean spirits; and they cast out many devils, and anointed with oil many that were sick, and healed them."—Mark 6:7, 13.

The elders are to anoint the sick. "Is any sick among you? let him call for the elders of the church; and let them pray over him, anointing him with oil in the name of the Lord: and the prayer of faith shall save the sick, and the Lord shall raise him up; and if he have committed sins they shall be forgiven him. Confess your faults one to another, and pray one for another, that ye may be healed. The effectual fervent prayer of a righteous man availeth much."—Jas. 5:14-16.

WHAT TO DO IN CASE THERE ARE NO ELDERS PRESENT.

Have others pray. "Again I say unto you, That if two of you shall agree on earth as touching anything that they shall ask, it shall be done for them of my Father which is in heaven. For where two or three are gathered together in my name, there am I in the midst of them."—Matt. 18:19, 20.

This uniting of two or more in prayer will apply not only to other things, but in case of sickness also. It is not always required that those so uniting be together in order to unite their prayer and faith. They may be at separate places, a thousand miles apart, and have a time set for special prayer, and God will honor the united faith and send an answer to the same. However, we have the promise also where two or three are gathered together in the name of Jesus that he is there in the midst of them.

While the laying on of hands is generally done by elders, yet the word as given in Mark 16:18, concerning laying hands on the sick, gives the liberty to those who believe, whether they are elders or not. We have witnessed the healing of the sick where children have laid on hands and offered up fervent prayers. It is our privilege, especially in cases of emergency, to lay our hands upon the sick who are in our midst, and ask God to do the healing. Or prayer may be offered without the laying on of hands and the healing done in answer to the prayer alone.

PROMISES WHEN ALONE.

IT often happens that believers are alone and in need of healing, or that there is no one else present to pray with the sick. In such cases there are some precious promises to inspire faith.

"If ye abide in me, and my words abide in you, ye shall ask what ye will, and it shall be done unto you."—Jno. 15:7.

"Beloved, if our heart condemn us not, then have we confidence toward God. And whatsoever we ask, we receive of him, because we keep his commandments, and do those things that are pleasing in his sight."—1 Jno. 3:21, 22.

"And this is the confidence that we have in him, that, if we ask anything according to his will, he heareth us: and if we know that he hear us, whatsoever we ask, we know that we have the petitions that we desired of him."—1 Jno. 5:14, 15.

"Is any among you afflicted? let him pray. Is any merry? let him sing psalms."—Jas. 5:13.

"Therefore, I say unto you, What things soever ye desire, when ye pray, believe that ye receive them, and ye shall have them."—Mark 11:24.

HANDKERCHIEFS MAY BE SENT.

There are times when people may have a very great desire to send for the elders or some one to come and pray for the sick, but circumstances are such as to make it almost impossible for them to do so or for the elders to come. It often happens, as it did with Paul, that ministers are engaged in a series of meetings and many calls come to visit the sick a great distance away, and they are unable to attend to their regular work and visit all the sick. In such cases either prayer alone may be offered, or handkerchiefs sent in the name of the Lord, to be laid upon the sick, instead of the laying on of hands. We read that "God wrought special miracles by the hands of Paul: so that from his body were brought unto the sick handkerchiefs or aprons, and the diseases departed from them, and the evil spirits went out of them."—Acts 19:11, 12. Many at the present time can testify to having received healing through the application of a handkerchief sent for that purpose.

A few years ago the wife of a brother became very sick. An elder was sent for, but through some cause could not come. While praying over the matter he felt led to lay his hands upon a handkerchief and send it in the name of the Lord to the afflicted one. The brother upon his arrival home, applied the handker. chief as directed, and the Lord sent his healing power immediately, and the woman was healed and raised up by the power of God. The handkerchief was laid away, and a few weeks later another member of the family was taken sick. The same handkerchief was applied to the sick one and prayer offered, and the healing power of the Lord was bestowed insomuch that the healing was instantaneous.

THE HEALING MAY OR MAY NOT BE IN-STANTANEOUS.

Many were healed instantly. "Now when the sun was setting, all they that had any sick with divers diseases brought them unto him; and he laid his hands on every one of them, and healed them. And devils also came out of many, crying out, and saying, Thou art Christ the Son of God. And he rebuking them suffered them not to speak: for they knew that he was Christ."—Luke 4:40, 41. "And by the hands of the apostles were many signs and wonders wrought among the people. . . . Insomuch that they brought forth the sick into the streets, and laid them on beds and couches, that at the least the shadow of Peter passing by might overshadow some of them. There came also a multitude out of the cities round about unto Jerusalem, bringing sick folks, and them which were vexed with unclean spirits: and they were healed every one."—Acts 5:12, 15, 16.

Palsied man—healed by faith of those who brought him. "And, behold, they brought to him a man sick of the palsy, lying on a bed: and Jesus seeing their faith said unto the sick of the palsy; Son, be of good cheer; thy sins be forgiven thee. And, behold, certain of the scribes said within themselves, this man blasphemeth. And Jesus knowing their thoughts said, Wherefore think ye evil in your hearts? For whether is easier, to say, Thy sins be forgiven thee; or to say, Arise and walk? But that ye may know that the Son of man hath power on earth to forgive sins, (then saith he to the sick of the palsy,) Arise, take up thy bed, and go unto thine house. And he arose, and departed unto his house."—Matt. 9:2-7.

The leper—healed by his own faith. "And, behold, there came a leper and worshiped him, saying, Lord, if thou wilt thou canst make me clean. And Jesus put forth his hand, and touched him, saying, I will; be thou clean. And immediately his leprosy was cleansed."—Matt. 8:2, 3.

The father of Publius—by the faith of Paul. "And it came to pass, that the father of Publius lay sick of a fever and of a bloody flux: to whom Paul entered in, and prayed, and laid his hands on him, and healed him."—Acts 28:8.

The servant—by the faith of the centurion. "And when Jesus was entered into Capernaum, there came unto him a centurion, beseeching him, and saying, Lord, my servant lieth at home sick of the palsy, grievously tormented. And Jesus said unto him, I will come and heal him. The centurion answered, and said, Lord, I am not worthy that thou shouldest come under my roof: but speak the word only, and my servant shall be healed. For I am a man under authority,

having soldiers under me: I say to this man, Go, and
he goeth; and to another, Come, and he cometh; and
to my servant, Do this, and he doeth it. When Jesus
heard it he marveled, and said to them that followed,
Verily, I say unto you, I have not found so great faith,
no, not in Israel. And I say unto you, That many
shall come from the east and west, and shall sit down
with Abraham, and Isaac, and Jacob, in the kingdom
of heaven: but the children of the kingdom shall be
cast out into outer darkness: there shall be weeping
and gnashing of teeth. And Jesus said unto the centurion, Go thy way; and as thou hast believed, so be
it done unto thee. And his servant was healed in the
selfsame hour."—Matt. 8:5-13.

The ten lepers—healed as they journeyed. "And as
he entered into a certain village, there met him ten
men that were lepers, which stood afar off: and they
lifted up their voices, and said, Jesus, Master, have
mercy on us. And when he saw them, he said unto
them, Go show yourselves unto the priests. And it
came to pass, that, as they went, they were cleansed."
—Luke 17:12-14.

Epaphroditus sick—God had mercy on him. "Yet
I supposed it necessary to send unto you Epaphroditus,
my brother, and companion in labor, and fellow soldier,
but your messenger, and he that ministered to my
wants. For he longed after you all, and was full of
heaviness, because that ye had heard that he had been
sick. For indeed he was sick nigh unto death: but

God had mercy on him; and not on him only, but on me also, lest I should have sorrow upon sorrow."— Phil. 2:25-27.

Some received handkerchiefs and aprons from Paul. "And God wrought special miracles by the hands of Paul: so that from his body were brought unto the sick handkerchiefs or aprons, and the diseases departed from them, and the evil spirits went out of them."— Acts 19:11, 12.

The blind man at first was not completely healed. "And he cometh to Bethsaida; and they bring a blind man unto him, and besought him to touch him. And he took the blind man by the hand, and led him out of the town; and when he had spit on his eyes, and put his hands upon him, he asked him if he saw aught. And he looked up, and said, I see men as trees, walking."—Mark 8:22-24.

Perfect healing of the blind man. "After that he put his hands again upon his eyes, and made him look up; and he was restored, and saw every man clearly." —Mark 8:25.

The nobleman believed—his son began to amend from that hour "So Jesus came again into Cana of Galilee, where he made the water wine. And there was a certain nobleman, whose son was sick at Capernaum. When he heard that Jesus was come out of Judea into Galilee, he went unto him, and besought him that he would come down, and heal his son: for he was at the point of death. Then said Jesus unto him, Except ye see signs and wonders ye will not believe. The noble-man saith unto him, Sir, come down ere my child die. Jesus saith unto him, Go thy way, thy son liveth. And the man believed the word that Jesus had spoken unto him, and he went his way. And as he was now going down, his servants met him, saying, Thy son liveth. Then inquired he of them the hour when he began to amend. And they said unto him, Yesterday at the seventh hour the fever left him. So the father knew that it was at the same hour, in the which Jesus said unto him, Thy son liveth: and himself believed, and his whole house."—Jno. 4:46-53.

Paul left Trophimus at Miletum sick. "Erastus abode at Corinth: but Trophimus have I left at Miletum sick."—2 Tim. 4:20. Because Paul left Trophimus sick and went on to another place, is no evidence whatever against divine healing. It does not prove that Paul did not have the gift of healing, neither does it prove that Trophimus was not healed. Whether Trophimus was or was not healed after Paul left would have been no evidence against divine healing. The word of God teaches us that it is appointed unto man once to die. Paul no doubt prayed for him, and prayed for him earnestly, and doubtless God heard and answered his prayer—probably healed him. The raising up from his sickness and the manifestation of the power of God in answer to Paul's prayer doubtless took place after Paul left. There may have been some good reasons for his not being instantly healed and immediately raised up as was the case with numbers of people for whom Paul had prayed before this time.

Doubtless the apostle prayed for many people who were not instantly healed and raised up; nevertheless the power of God was manifested in and through them, and the name of the Lord glorified. If one who is sick is prayed for, and is not instantly raised up, but becomes well as soon as he would were he under the care of a physician, can we not give God glory for the manifestation of his healing power, the same as we would give honor or praise to a physician who would successfully treat a severe case of sickness? It is too often the case that people fail to give God glory in such cases and consider, although no medicine whatever is given, that it can not be called a case of divine healing. While in the majority of the cases of sickness recorded in the New Testament the healings were instantaneous, and the sick made well immediately, yet such was not always the case; neither is it always the case at the present time. And we should give God glory, and render honor to whom honor is due, and magnify the name of the Lord for his wonderful works.

IMPORTUNITY.

When coming to the Lord for special help, whether for healing or some other thing in accordance with his will, if we do not receive that for which we ask, by way of the manifestation of his power or by witness of his Spirit that he has heard and will grant it unto us, we should continue with importunity; or in other words, we should continue until we do become satisfied regarding the same. There are many instances mentioned in the Bible of those who have plead with God until they received the proper answer. We read of how Jacob wrestled with the angel all night long. We read of the importunity and earnest prayer of our blessed Master in the garden of Gethsemane, how he prayed, went again the second time, and the third time, saying the same words, making the same petition; and God sent an angel who strengthened him, and he received that help which was needed.

Blind Bartimeus. "And they came to Jericho: and as he went out of Jericho with his disciples and a great number of people, blind Bartimeus, the son of Timeus, sat by the highway-side begging. And when he heard that it was Jesus of Nazareth, he began to cry out, and say, Jesus, thou son of David, have mercy on me. And many charged him that he should hold his peace: but he cried the more a great deal, Thou Son of David, have mercy on me. And Jesus stood still, and commanded him to be called. And they call the blind man, saying unto him, Be of good comfort, arise; he calleth thee. And he, casting away his garment, rose, and came to Jesus. And Jesus answered and said unto him, What wilt thou that I should do unto thee? The blind man said unto him, Lord, that I might receive my sight. And Jesus said unto him, Go thy way; thy faith hath made thee whole. And immediately he received his sight, and followed Jesus in the way."— Mark 10:46-52.

Two blind men. "And when Jesus departed from thence, two blind men followed him, crying, and saying, Thou Son of David, have mercy on us. And when he was come into the house, the blind men came to him: and Jesus saith unto them, Believe ye that I am able to do this? They said unto him, Yea, Lord. Then touched he their eyes saying, According to your faith be it unto you. And their eyes were opened; and Jesus straitly charged them, saying, See that no man know it. But they, when they were departed, spread abroad his fame in all that country."—Matt. 9:27-31.

Woman of Canaan. "And, behold a woman of Canaan came out of the same coasts, and cried unto him, saying, Have mercy on me, O Lord, Thou Son of David; my daughter is grievously vexed with a devil. But he answered her not a word. And his disciples came and besought him, saying, Send her away; for she crieth after us. But he answered and said, I am not sent but unto the lost sheep of the house of Israel. Then came she and worshiped him, saying, Lord, help me. But he answered and said, It is not meet to take the children's bread, and to cast it to dogs. And she said, Truth, Lord: yet the dogs eat of the crumbs that fall from their master's table. Then Jesus answered and said unto her, O woman, great is thy faith: be it unto thee even as thou wilt. And her daughter was made whole from that very hour."—Matt. 15:22-28.

A WOMAN SUFFERED OF PHYSICIANS.

"AND a certain woman which had an issue of blood twelve years, and had suffered many things of many physicians, and had spent all that she had, and was nothing bettered, but rather grew worse."—Mark 5:25, 26. This woman had suffered "many things of many physicians," and yet she was no better, but rather grew worse. Thousands of people to-day can give the same testimony. Luke in speaking of this woman, said, she "had spent all her living upon physicians, neither could be healed of any."—Luke 8:43.

She was healed by faith. "When she had heard of Jesus, came in the press behind, and touched his gar-ment. For she said, If I may touch but his clothes, I shall be whole. And straightway the fountain of her blood was dried up, and she felt in her body that she was healed of that plague. And Jesus, immediately knowing in himself that virtue had gone out of him, turned him about in the press, and said, Who touched my clothes? And his disciples said unto him, Thou seest the multitude thronging thee, and sayest thou, Who touched me? And he looked round about to see her that had done this thing. But the woman fearing and trembling, knowing what was done in her, came and fell down before him, and told him all the truth. And he said unto her, Daughter, thy faith hath made thee whole; go in peace, and be whole of thy plague.''—Mark 5:27-34. When she came to Jesus with such implicit faith and confidence, he said unto her, "Daughter, be of good comfort: thy faith hath made thee whole; go in peace.''

We read of some one else who did not trust his case in the hands of the Lord, but trusted to the physicians, and for that reason died. "And Asa in the thirty and ninth year of his reign was diseased in his feet, until his disease was exceeding great: yet in his disease he sought not to the Lord, but to the physicians. And Asa slept with his fathers, and died in the one and fortieth year of his reign.''—2 Chron. 16:12, 13.

INSTRUCTIONS TO US.

IT is often said by unbelievers, doubters, and those who do not trust in the Lord for their needed help, that the day of healing is past, and what was written in the New Testament concerning divine healing was written only for the apostles and the people of their day. But we are glad to know that such is not the case. While they had these privileges, yet it was not for them alone. It was written for the children of God and those who would come to him in faith believ-

ing.   It is the privilege of the people to-day, just as
much as it was almost nineteen centuries ago, to come
to the Lord in faith believing and receive pardon and
enjoy the peace of God.   They also have the same
privileges as did people of olden times, of coming for
the healing of their bodies.   They must come with
prayer, in faith believing, and the promise is that it
shall be according to their faith.

If we have not the same privileges regarding the
healing of our bodies as had the people in the days of
the apostles, then the word of God is of no use to us,
any more than a history of the past to tell what people
did centuries ago, and for us to learn of their privileges.
If such is the case, then there is no hope for our salvation.   We can receive no help to our souls through the
word of God.   But we are glad to know that Jesus is
still seeking out the lost, and healing all those who
are oppressed of the devil; as we read, "How God
anointed Jesus of Nazareth with the Holy Ghost and
with power: who went about doing good, and healing
all that were oppressed of the devil; for God was with
him."—Acts 10:38.   Not only did he heal the sick,
but "to him give all the prophets witness, that
through his name whosoever believeth in him shall
receive remission of sins."—Ver. 43.   And to the children of God he gives the precious promises of deliverance and power over the power of the enemy.   And
furthermore he says, "There hath no temptation taken
you but such as is common to man: but God is faith-

6

ful, who will not suffer you to be tempted above that ye are able: but will with the temptation also make a way to escape, that ye may be able to bear it."—1 Cor. 10:13.

James instructs us to pray one for another for healing in time of sickness (Jas. 5:16), and also advises the sending for elders. Nowhere in the New Testament are found any instructions advising the sending for a physician, or giving of medicines. In case of an accident or injury, where skill is needed to replace bones or dress wounds, or something of that character, there is nothing objectionable in procuring aid on that line, and asking the Lord to do the healing. But as far as disease and sickness are concerned, it is one of the privileges of the children of God to be healed of all manner of sickness and all manner of disease, the same to-day as the people were in the days of the apostles.

MEANS TO BE USED.

"Is any among you afflicted? let him pray. Is any merry? let him sing psalms. Is any sick among you? let him call for the elders of the church; and let them pray over him, anointing him with oil in the name of the Lord: and the prayer of faith shall save the sick, and the Lord shall raise him up; and if he have committed sins, they shall be forgiven him. Confess your faults one to another, and pray one for another, that ye may be healed. The effectual fervent prayer of a righteous man availeth much."—Jas. 5:13-16. "And these signs shall follow them that believe: In my name shall they cast out devils; they shall speak with new tongues; they shall take up serpents; and if they drink any deadly thing it shall not hurt them; they shall lay hands on the sick, and they shall recover."—Mark 16:17, 18.

We learn by this that the means to be used in case of sickness is anointing with oil, laying on of hands, and prayer. Faith must accompany these things. The prayer of faith must be offered, and the one who comes with such confidence will receive what is promised in the Word. The elders or any others who have the gifts of healing to go forth with such authority, can be assured that the signs will follow, as mentioned in the word of God. It is not always necessary to anoint with oil, it is not always necessary to lay on hands; yet we find that the apostles anointed many with oil, who were healed (Mark 6:13), and very often laid hands on the sick. Jesus himself at one time, when many sick people were brought unto him, laid hands on every one of them and healed them. Luke 4:40.

PRIVILEGES NOT TAKEN FROM THE CHURCH.

WHEN Jesus sent his disciples forth to preach the gospel, he endued them with power from on high. This heavenly unction and qualification fitted them to preach the gospel in a way that would convince sinners and enable as many to be saved as would heed the words of the Lord.   It also qualified them to go forth and pray for the sick, laying hands upon them when necessary, for the healing of their sicknesses and diseases.   We find these signs followed believers during the time of the apostles, as recorded in the New Testament.   And according to history we learn that the same was continued even after the death of the apostles, accordingly as the people followed the teachings of the word of God.

A few centuries after the day of Pentecost we find that people had drifted away from the truth into a great apostasy.   As they did so they were shorn of their strength, like Samson, who, when he yielded to the cunning devices of Delilah and had his hair shorn, was also shorn of his strength insomuch that he was unable to break the withs as before and defeat the plans of the Philistines.   He was placed under bondage to his enemies and persecuted until he was blind. Likewise those who departed from the faith fell a prey unto their enemies, were blinded to the truth, and led into the ways of error—were shorn of their strength until the signs did not follow them.

We truly can thank God that we live in the time when Zion, the church of the living God, is returning to her primitive beauty and power, when God is raising up men and women, anointing them by the Spirit for his service in gathering together his elect from the four

winds of the earth, preaching the gospel in all its purity
by the Holy Ghost sent down from heaven. As the
demonstration of the Spirit is manifested in the
preaching of the gospel, the signs follow as in days of
old, and the glory of God rests upon his people.

It is manifest to all that the doctrine of Jesus Christ
has not changed, but Jesus Christ is the same yesterday, and to-day, and forever; and fulfilling Jas. 5:14,
15 is present truth. And the words of Jude is an
exhortation worthy our consideration, when he said,
"Beloved, when I gave all diligence to write unto
you of the common salvation, it was needful for me to
write unto you, and exhort you that ye should earnestly contend for the faith once delivered unto the
saints."—Jude 3. "Only let your conversation be as
it becometh the gospel of Christ: that whether I come
and see you, or else be absent, I may hear of your
affairs, that ye stand fast in one spirit, with one mind
striving together for the faith of the gospel."—Phil.
1:27. "Fight the good fight of faith, lay hold on eter-
nal life, whereunto thou art also called, and hast pro-
fessed a good profession before many witnesses."—1
Tim. 6:12.

"IS ANY SICK AMONG YOU?"

"Is any sick among you? let him call for the elders
of the church; and let them pray over him anointing

him with oil in the name of the Lord; and the prayer of faith shall save the sick, and the Lord shall raise him up; and if he have committed sins they shall be forgiven him. Confess your faults one to another, and pray one for another that ye may be healed. The effectual fervent prayer of a righteous man availeth much."—Jas. 5:14-16.

These words were spoken to the children of God and clearly set forth their privileges in Christ Jesus. But there is more included in the words "Is any sick among you?" than may be perceived. It truly shows forth that if there are any of God's children sick they can obey the Word by sending for the elders, being anointed, prayed for, and healed. These instructions should be carried out by the children of God; that is, to take the Bible way in time of sickness. When Jesus spoke the words in Mark 16:15-18 and said, "These signs shall follow them that believe," he meant that such would be the case in the church as long as there were any true believers. His power to us is only limited by our faith.

As divine healing is something that is very greatly opposed, generally by unbelievers, it often happens in families that the father is saved and the mother is an unbeliever, or the mother is a child of God and the father is an unbeliever, and in case the children are sick the unbelieving one is opposed to trusting the children in the hands of God for healing. It therefore often happens that the one who is a child of God must submit to earthly help and remedies, contrary to his or her desire; but where such is unavoidable God does not impute it as sin. However, even if one of the parents may be an unbeliever, or even an opposer, the other one can go into the secret closet and with an earnest fervent prayer prevail upon God to bestow his healing power, and he will grant the same according to the faith of the one sending up the petition.

There are people who feel they can trust God for themselves, but are afraid to trust him fully with their children, and are sometimes made to believe that there is nothing in the word of God concerning an example of such. But we find the woman of Canaan was not only willing to trust her daughter in the hands of the Lord for healing, but with such earnest petitions implored him to heal her daughter that the Master was moved with great compassion. She would not be put off without an answer; she would not be turned aside except the answer were a favorable one. She went forth with importunity and earnest pleadings until the Master turned and spoke the words in accordance with the desire of her heart; and her daughter was made whole.

The man who came to Jesus with his son who had a deaf and dumb spirit from the time he was a little child, was not willing to return until the child was made well. Even then Jesus required faith on the part of the father, and encouraged him by saying, "If thou canst believe"; and straightway the father of the child cried out, and said with tears, "Lord, I believe: help thou mine unbelief." Jesus then cast out the deaf and dumb spirit, and the child was made well.

Another case recorded wherein a child was committed unto the Lord for healing was the daughter of Jairus, the ruler of the synagogue. She was very sick. He came to Jesus in her behalf. Soon after messengers were sent to tell him not to trouble the Master, for the child was dead. But Jesus urged him to trust the child in his hands, and required faith on the part of the father, saying, "Fear not: believe only, and she shall be made whole." The father trusted in the words of Jesus, and his daughter though dead was raised to life again and restored to health.

SINNERS MAY BE HEALED AND FORGIVEN.

THE words "Is any sick among you?" may include all who have faith enough to send for the elders, whether saint or sinner, and the privilege extended to the sinners is, "If ye have committed sins, they shall be forgiven him."—Jas. 5:15. It was a sinner that was brought to Jesus by his friends, and healed of the palsy. This man was not only healed, but his sins were forgiven. "And behold, they brought unto him a man sick of the palsy, lying on a bed: and Jesus seeing their faith said unto the sick of the palsy: Son, be of good cheer; thy sins be forgiven thee. And, behold, certain of the scribes said within themselves, This man blasphemeth. And Jesus knowing their thoughts said, Wherefore think ye evil in your hearts? For whether is easier, to say, Thy sins be forgiven thee; or to say, Arise, and walk. But that ye may know that the Son of man hath power on earth to forgive sins, (then saith he to the sick of the palsy,) Arise, take up thy bed, and go unto thine own house. And he arose, and departed to his house. But when the multitudes saw it, they marveled, and glorified God, which had given such power unto men."—Matt. 9:2-8.

"Now there is at Jerusalem by the sheep market a pool, which is called in the Hebrew tongue Bethesda, having five porches. In these lay a great multitude of impotent folk, of blind, halt, withered, waiting for the moving of the water. For an angel went down at a certain season into the pool, and troubled the water: whosoever then first after the troubling of the water stepped in was made whole of whatsoever disease he had. And a certain man was there which had an infirmity thirty and eight years. When Jesus saw him lie, and knew that he had now been a long time in that case, he saith unto him, Wilt thou be made whole? The impotent man answered him, Sir, I have no man, when the water is troubled, to put me into the pool: but while I am coming, another steppeth down before me. Jesus saith unto him, Rise, take up thy bed, and walk. And immediately the man was made whole, and took up his bed, and walked: and on the same day was the Sabbath. The Jews therefore said unto him that was cured, It is the Sabbath day: it is not lawful for thee to carry thy bed. He answered them, He that made me whole, the same said unto me, Take up thy bed, and walk. Then asked they him, What man is that which said unto thee, Take up thy bed, and walk? And he that was healed wist not who it was: for Jesus had conveyed himself away, a multitude being in that place. Afterward Jesus findeth him in the temple, and said unto him, Behold, thou art made whole: sin no more, lest a worse thing come unto thee.''—Jno. 5:2-14.

There were many sinners among the multitude of sick who came to Jesus, of whom Luke says, "He laid his hands on every one of them, and healed them." Some of them were sinners, because the Word says, "And devils also came out of many."—Luke 4:40, 41. The signs were to follow believers among sinners, because where it says, "They shall lay hands on the sick, and they shall recover," it also says, "In my name shall they cast out devils." If through the aid of believers devils may be cast out of sinners, truly the healing power will also be manifested among them. In setting forth the word of God to the people sinners should be made to realize that in time of trouble, perplexity, and sickness, it is their privilege to come to the children of God for instruction and help in the ways of the Lord, for the salvation of their souls, and the healing of their bodies.

HIS POWER, ABILITY, AND WILLINGNESS.

JESUS still has the power, ability, and willingness to heal all who ask in faith believing. Are you desiring to launch out in the ways of the divine life and trust in the Lord for the healing of your body, as well as for the keeping of your soul? If so, do not be afraid to trust him, because he is abundantly able to help you. He has not become weakened, but is all-powerful; yea, he still has all power in heaven and on earth. Do not be afraid of his inability to help you in every time of need, to handle your case whatever the trouble may be; for we read that he is able to do exceeding abundantly above all that we ask or think. Do not be afraid concerning his willingness, as he is willing to help all who come unto him, and says, "Come unto me, all ye that labor and are heavy laden, and I will give you rest. Take my yoke upon you, and learn of me; for I am meek and lowly in heart: and ye shall find rest unto your souls. For my yoke is easy, and my burden is light."—Matt. 11:28-30.

He will not only help concerning your soul, but has power to "heal all manner of sickness and all manner of disease," and "over all the power of the enemy." Furthermore he says, "Therefore I say unto you, What things soever ye desire when ye pray, believe that ye receive them, and ye shall have them."—Mark 11:24. "And this is the confidence that we have in him, that, if we ask anything according to his will, he heareth us:

and if we know that he hear us, whatsoever we ask, we know that we have the petitions that we desired of him."—1 Jno. 5:14, 15.

May the Lord "grant you according to the riches of his glory, to be strengthened with might by his Spirit in the inner man; that Christ may dwell in your hearts by faith; that ye, being rooted and grounded in love, may be able to comprehend with all saints what is the breadth, and length, and depth, and height; and to know the love of Christ, which passeth knowledge, that ye might be filled with all the fullness of God. Now unto him that is able to do exceeding abundantly above all that we can ask or think, according to the power that worketh in us, unto him be glory in the church by Christ Jesus throughout all ages, world without end.   Amen."—Eph. 3:16-21.   "Jesus Christ the same yesterday, and to-day, and forever."— Heb. 13:8.

APPENDIX.

A time of healing prophesied. Isa. 35:5, 6.

A prophecy of Christ the healer. Isa. 53:3-5.

His birth. Matt. 1:21.

Fulfillment of the prophecy. Matt. 8:16, 17; 1 Pet. 2:24; Luke 7:21, 22.

Jesus had the power of healing. Matt. 28:18; Acts 10:38.

He exercised that power. Matt. 4:23, 24; 8:17; Luke 4:40, 41.

He taught and practiced healing from the beginning of his ministry. Matt. 4:23.

He gave that power to the twelve. Matt. 10:1.

They exercised that power. Mark 16:20; Acts 5:12-16.

He gave that power to the seventy. Luke 10:1-9.

They exercised that power. Luke 10:17-20.

He gave that power to Stephen, Paul, and others. Acts 6:8; 14:8-10; 28:8.

That power is given to some in the church. 1 Cor. 12:9.

That power is given to the elders. Jas. 5:14, 15.

That power is given us if we believe. Mark 16:16-18; Jno. 14:12.

Faith was required of those desiring healing. Matt. 9:29; Mark 5:25-34; Mark 5:36.

Some were healed through the faith of others. Matt. 8:5, 13; Jno. 4:50; Matt. 9:2; Mark 9:23.

Those who pray must have faith. Matt. 21:22; Heb. 11:6; Jas. 1:6, 7; Acts 6:8; Jas. 5:15; Mark 11:24.

The day of healing is not past with believers. Mark 16:16-18.

All things are possible to him that believeth. Mark 9:23.

We must believe when we pray. Mark 11:24.

We must have confidence in him. 1 Jno. 5:14.

How we know he will answer. 1 Jno. 5:15; 3:22; Mark 11:23, 24; Matt. 21:21, 22.

What to do when afflicted. Jas. 5:13.

What to do in case of sickness. Jas. 5:14.

What must the elders do? Jas. 5:14.

The prayer of faith must be offered. Jas. 5:15.

What is sometimes required of the sick? Jas. 5:16; Acts 14:9; Mark 5:34; Matt. 9:29.

Others must have faith in case the sick are unable to exercise faith. Mark 9:23, 24; Jas. 5:15; Matt. 9:2.

What must accompany faith? Jas. 2:17, 18.

What are the works?

> Where there are faults, confess them. Jas. 5:13-16.
>
> Works of the centurion—came to Jesus. Matt. 8:5-10.
>
> Works of the man with the withered hand—he stretched it forth. Matt. 12:13.
>
> Works of the lame man—looked and arose. Acts 3:4, 6.
>
> Works of the woman with an issue of blood—touched his garment. Mark 5:27, 28.
>
> Works of the ten lepers—showed themselves to the priests. Luke 17:14.

Works of the blind man—washed in the pool of
Siloam. Jno. 9:7.

Works of Naaman the leper—washed in the river
Jordan. 2 Kings 5:10, 14.

The laying on of hands.

Jesus laid hands on the sick. Luke 4:40; Mark
6:5.

He took Jairus' daughter by the hand. Mark
5:23, 41.

He put his hands twice on the eyes of the blind
man. Mark 8:23, 25.

He laid hands on the crooked woman. Luke 13:
11-13.

He touched the ear of the servant of the high
priest. Luke 22:51.

He touched the deaf man. Mark 7:32, 33.

Ananias laid hands on Saul. Acts 9:17, 18.

Paul laid hands on the father of Publius. Acts
28:8.

Peter raised Dorcas. Acts 9:41.

The apostles laid on hands. Mark 16:15, 18, 20.

Them that believe shall lay on hands. Mark 16:
17, 18.

Anointing with oil.

The apostles anointed the sick. Mark 6:7, 13.

The elders are to anoint the sick. Jas. 5:14.

What to do in case there are no elders present.

Have others pray for the sick. Matt. 18:19;
Mark 16:16-18.

Promises in case no one else is present to pray.　Jas.
5:13; Mark 11:24; Jno. 15:7; 1 Jno. 3:22; 1 Jno.
5:14, 15.

In special cases handkerchiefs may be sent.　Acts 19:12.

The healing may or may not be instantaneous.

Many were healed instantly.　Luke 4:40; Acts 5:16.

Palsied man—by faith of those who brought him.
Matt. 9:2.

The leper—by his own faith.　Matt. 8:2.

The father of Publius—by the faith of Paul.　Acts
28:8.

The servant—by the faith of the centurion. Matt.
8:13.

The ten lepers were healed as they journeyed.
Luke 17:14.

Epaphroditus sick—God had mercy on him.
Phil. 2:27.

Some received handkerchiefs and aprons from
Paul.　Acts 19:12.

The blind man at first was not completely healed.
Mark 8:23, 24.

Perfect healing of the blind man.　Mark 8:25.

The nobleman believed—his son began to amend
from that hour.　Jno. 4:50, 52.

Paul left Trophimus at Miletum sick. 2 Tim. 4:20

Importunity.

Blind Bartimeus.　Mark 10:46-52.

Two blind men.　Matt. 9:27-31.

The woman of Canaan.　Matt. 15:22-28.

A woman suffered many things of physicians. Mark 5:26.

> She was healed by faith. Mark 5:34.

Instructions to us—prayer and sending for elders. Jas. 5:13, 14.

Means to be used—anointing with oil, laying on of hands, and prayer of faith. Jas. 5:14, 15; Mark 16:18.

This privilege has not been taken from the church. Heb. 3:8; Jas. 5:15; Jude 3.

"Is any sick among you?"—includes all who have faith enough to send for the elders—saint or sinner. Jas. 5:14, 15.

Sinners may be healed and forgiven. Jas. 5:15; Luke 4:41; Matt. 9:2-6.

Jesus still has the power, ability, and willingness to heal all who ask in faith believing. Heb. 13:8; Eph. 3:20, 21.

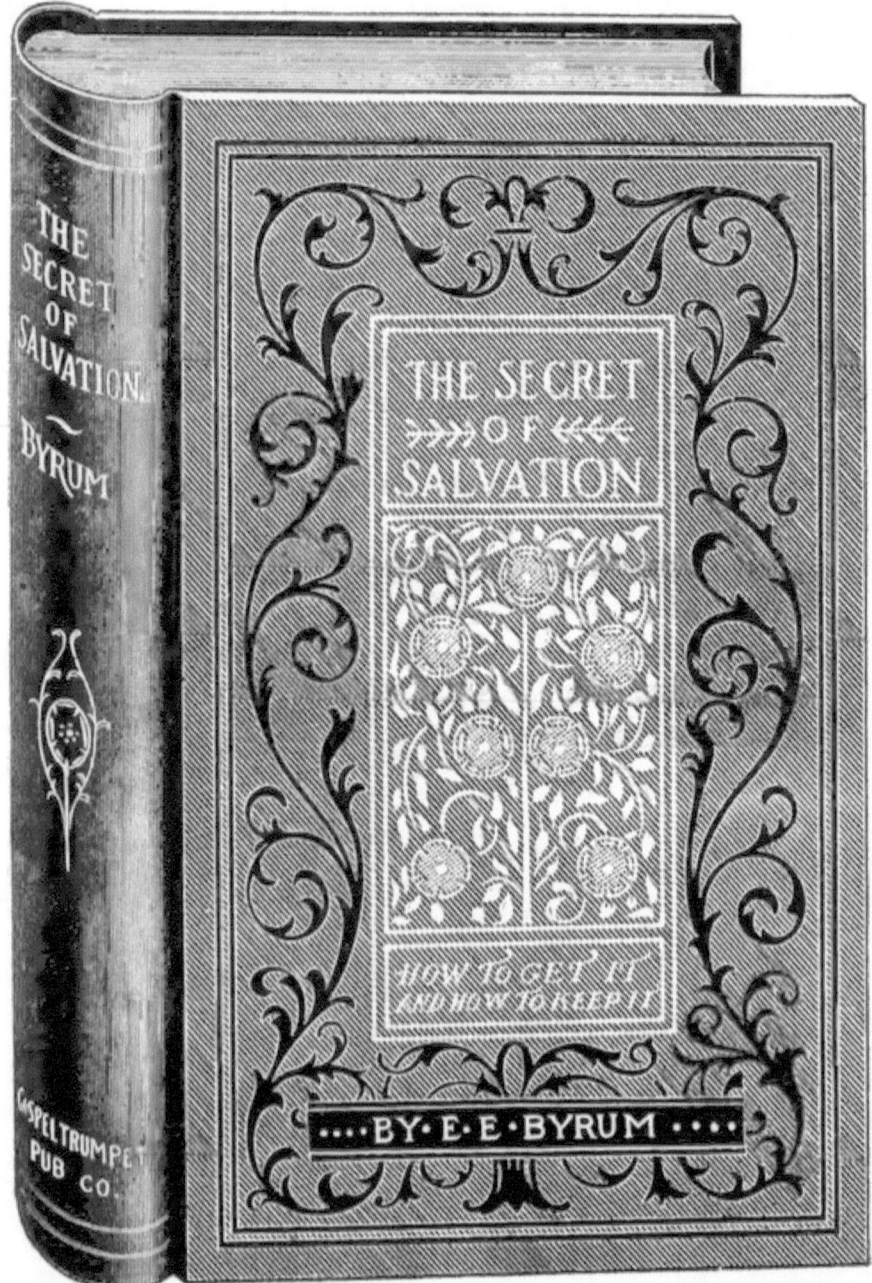

The Secret of Salvation:

How to Get It, and How to Keep It.

....BY E. E. BYRUM....

CONTENTS.

Salvation; What it Means; Whence it Comes; Who Can Have it? The Secret of Salvation; . . . How to Keep Salvation; Prayer; Prevailing Prayer; How to Make the Lord Hear; How to Make the Lord Answer; The Prayer of Faith; Its Effects; Agreement in Prayer; Why Prayer is not Answered; Keeping in Line with God; Faith; The Trial of Faith; Severe Testings; Faith and Trust; Spiritual Tests; Tests for Temporal Things; A forward Move; The First Difficulties; Supposed Hindrances; Temptations; How to Overcome Them; Fiery Trials and their Benefits; Kept by His Power; Counting all Things Joy; The Gospel of Healing; The Commission; To the Patriarchs; To the Prophets; To the Apostles; To Believers; To Whom Given Now; Promises Given; Healing of Diseases; The Healing Faith; Who can Have it; Who can be Healed; Why it has not been Universally Taught; Devils Cast Out; Miracles Wrought; Healing of the Blind; Deaf and Dumb Healed; Broken Bones Healed; Means Used in Healing; What to Do in Case of Sickness; Hezekiah's Figs; Timothy's Wine; Paul's Thorn; Luke, the Physician; Hindrances to Healing; How to Remove Hindrances; Contending for the Faith.

OVER 400 PAGES. ❧ 110 CHAPTERS.

Cloth Binding,	-	-	-	-	$1.00
Paper Cover,	-	-	-	-	.35

DIVINE HEALING 🍃 🍃
🍃 🍃 OF SOUL AND BODY.

BY E. E. BYRUM.

The author shows that the body as well as the soul
can be healed by Divine Power.   That the day of miracles is not past, but the "signs will follow them that
believe."

Part 1 teaches Divine Healing of the soul from sin,
and how to bring it into proper relationship with God,
where faith can be exercised for the healing of the
body.

Part 2 teaches Divine Healing of the body.   The
following chapters are especially interesting: The Doctrine of Healing, Is the Day of Healing Past? The Use
of Medicine, Means which God Blesses, The Prayer of
Faith, Can I be Healed? Hindrances to Healing.

Part 3 consists of testimonies from those who have
been healed by divine power.   More than fifty wonderful testimonies are given from those who have been
healed of fevers, heart disease, tumors, cancers, con-
sumption, insanity, nervous prostration, and broken
bones, as well as from those who have had their blind
eyes opened, etc., showing that when the conditions
are fully complied with, healing will follow.

This book has been read by thousands who have followed its instructions, and as a result are to-day well
and happy.

Substantially Bound in Cloth,	-	$1.00
Same in Paper Cover,	- -	.25

The Grace of Healing; ❧ ❧
❧ ❧ or, Christ Our Physician.

BY J. W. BYERS. A companion to "Divine Healing of Soul and Body." Contains 342 pages.

This is a new book containing authentic information on the subject of Divine Healing. The author clearly sets forth the fact that Divine Healing is a privilege to be enjoyed by all who believe. Divine Healing in prophecy is presented in a beautiful manner. First the prophecy, then its fulfillment; not only in the days of Christ and his apostles, but it is shown how the gifts of healing were placed in the church never to be withdrawn, and the work is still going on.

His chapters on Prayer, Importunity, Faith, How to Retain Healing, Conversion and Healing, Does Sickness Come from God? and Fifteen Objections Answered are full of interest and information. One chapter is devoted to the "Mystery of Iniquity" and its workings. Some of the greatest delusions of modern times are exposed, and very interesting questions are answered; such as Can Satan Afflict People? Is it possible for him to heal and perform miracles? What are the lying wonders to which the scripture refers? etc. This book bears a message of hope and comfort to all, but especially to those who are afflicted and in a suffering condition. You can not read it without having your faith strengthened, your courage increased, and your hope renewed.

Strongly Bound in Cloth,	-	-	$1.00
Same in Paper Cover, -	-	-	.35

Letters of Love & Counsel for "Our Girls"

JENNIE C. RUTTY

Letters of Love And

Counsel for "Our Girls."

.....By Jennie C. Rutty.....

A beautiful and valuable book written especially for girls, by a Christian mother who through years of experience and observation has accumulated precious information on many points about which girls need to be instructed. Everywhere snares and pitfalls are set to entrap the innocent feet of our girls, and lead them astray. The wise counsel, friendly admonitions, and words of warning which are given in this book will serve to fortify them against the tricks of the enemy, and guide their feet in the "better way." To those who have already been led into error, its words of sweet consolation will inspire new hope, and cheer them up to renewed efforts toward a life of purity and happiness. The subject matter is arranged in the form of letters to the girls, any one of which is worth more than the price of the entire book.

"A collection of letters on subjects of vital importance to growing girls, written in a tender, personal way that will appeal to the hearts of those whom its author hopes to reach. It is a book that every wise mother should place in the hands of the daughter that she would send forth in life girded for the fray, with an enlightened understanding."—*The Union Signal.*

331 PAGES.

Nicely bound in Cloth, $1.00
Same in Paper Cover,   -   .35

MOTHERS' COUNSEL

❧ ❧ ❧ ❧ TO THEIR SONS.

By Jennie C. Rutty.

Companion to "Letters of Love and Counsel for 'Our Girls,'" and bound in the same style.

A new and valuable book devoted especially to the interests of our boys and young men. The information which it contains is also of great value to older persons. Its mission is to save our boys from following the pathway which leads downward, and to induce them to live upright, pure, and beautiful lives. It hoists the "danger signals" along the way and sounds a note of warning at points where the enemy usually lies in wait to capture and deceive. The results of wrong living are vividly pictured to the mind, as is also the reward which comes to those who choose the right. In this book you will find originality. There is a departure from the old beaten track, and new territory is explored. A Christian mother talks to the boys, telling them many things she has learned by careful observation and years of experience. The information contained in her talks on the Tobacco Habit, Intemperance, and Courtship and Marriage are priceless. The author's direct and familiar way of addressing the boys, together with the interesting testimonials which she has introduced, can not fail to command the attention and hold the interest of every honest boy, young man, or older person who reads this book.

436 Pages. ❧ ❧ Price, $1.00.

The Better Testament;

...or the...

Two Testaments Compared.

SHOWING THE SUPERIORITY OF THE GOSPEL OVER THE LAW
OF MOSES ACCORDING TO THE EPISTLES OF PAUL,
ESPECIALLY THAT ADDRESSED TO THE HEBREWS.

.....BY WM. G. SCHELL.....

This is the title-page of the larger volume of "THE
BETTER TESTAMENT," which is now in the
hands of the printers, and will be ready for the market
soon after Jan. 1, 1900. It treats thoroughly the following subjects: The Two laws; The Two Covenants;
Salvation by Works; Salvation by Faith; The Law of
Bondage; The Law of Liberty; The Gospel in the Old
Testament; The Law in the New Testament; Repentance; Justification; The New Birth; Holy Living;
Consecration; Sanctification; Holiness; The Types
and Antitypes of the Bible; The Atonement; Marriage
and Divorcement; The Church of Moses; The Church
of Christ; Divine Healing; The Tithing Sytem; The
New Jerusalem; and many other subjects of vital
importance. Every subject is treated first from the
standpoint of the Old Testament then from that of the
New Testament, thus enabling the reader to comprehend fully the difference between the two Testaments.
No Bible student's library will be complete without it.
The book will contain about 450 pages.

CLOTH,   -   -   - $1.00

HALF MOROCCO, -   -   1.50

The Gospel Trumpet.

E. E. BYRUM, Editor.

An eight-page Weekly Religious Journal, having for its object the spread of the pure gospel. It is devoted to the principles of holiness, full salvation, and the oneness of God's people, and opposes all forms of division among Christians. No creed is upheld. It also gives interpretations of prophecy, testimonies of Divine Healing and of remarkable answers to prayer, etc. Secular advertisements are not admitted to its columns. Sample copies mailed free.

Subscription one year, $1.00. Six Months, 50c. Three months, 25c.

Die Evangeliums Posaune.

A four-page Semi-monthly Religious Journal **Published in German.** In its teaching it is similar to The Gospel Trumpet, both presenting the doctrine of full salvation of both soul and body.

Subscription one year, $1.00. Six months, 50c. Three months, 25c.

The Shining Light.

....A PAPER FOR CHILDREN....

It contains beautiful Bible stories, gems of poetry, and interesting articles on various subjects which both please and instruct the children. Each issue contains one or more pictures, which enable its little readers to form correct ideas of the subjects represented. It also contains little testimonies of full salvation and divine healing. Published weekly.

Subscription one year, 25c.

Subscription Rates to Sunday-Schools.

Ten copies, three months (to one address), - -	$0	50
Twenty-five copies, three months (to one address), -	1	15
Fifty copies, three mouths (to one address), - -	2	00

www.ingramcontent.com/pod-product-compliance
Lightning Source LLC
Chambersburg PA
CBHW022341020726
47500CB00004B/1227